In Reindeer Hide

A novel by

Matti Aikio

Translated by John Weinstock

Set in Adobe Jensen Pro

The original of this book was published as

I Dyreskind
Fortælling
fra Finmarken
Roman
Forlagt av H. Aschehoug & Co.
(W. Nygaard) • Kristiania 1906

Cover design by John Weinstock and Beth Brotherton

Ollu giitu dáid olbmuide hui buori veahki ovddas:
Reidar Rødland, Harald Gaski, Britt Rajala,
Elina Helander-Renvall ja Sonja Siltala.

Lilienskiold illustrations appear courtesy of the
Archives: Finnmark County Library.

This translation has been published with
the financial support of NORLA.

In Reindeer Hide

In Memorium

Faith Fjeld

Bohccot (reindeer)

I

The courtroom in the little Sámi town was full to the last seat. The platform inside the bar was no larger than that it could barely hold the bailiff, the two attorneys and the interpreter.

Biettar Oula and his wife stood leaning against the bar, elegantly dressed as if they were the objects of a bridal speech – and not of an aggressive cross examination concerning a reindeer theft.

Lasse, the one originally indicted, was squatting in one of the two small detention rooms and had his ear right by the keyhole trying to catch one or other word of the farmer's testimony. He had suddenly begun to make trouble this morning, and the case had become difficult and taken a dangerous turn for Biettar Oula.

"Six female reindeer," whispered a man standing near the detention door and in a seemingly enthusiastic conversation with his neighbor. "Six female reindeer," he repeated one more time. And Lasse was no dumber than that he understood immediately it was a new offer from Biettar Oula. He smacked his lips. Well … Anyway you learned Norwegian and good manners at the institution in Trondhjem. The city itself was worth seeing, he had heard. And the jail was quite light and friendly, at any rate compared to this dark, dirty hole.

— The temporary and rather young bailiff looked inquiringly at Biettar Oula. "Tell me – how can it be that in the course of a few years you have been able to work your way up to the district's richest Sámi herder?"

Biettar Oula smiled shyly and patted his black and, for a Sámi, unusually thick beard. "I take care of my herd," he said. He had an instinctive feeling that a little boast in all innocence would give his word the impression of trustworthiness. "The heat from the stove down here in the village, thank God, has not yet become so valued by me that I would leave the herd to the hired hands – as it seems the custom has become in recent times." His eyelids which otherwise were full of bold insight remained valiantly in the most innocent folds. It looked like he had no idea that the bailiff was trying to set a trap for him.

Fully understanding that clothes make the man, he had dressed in a black reindeer coat of the finest reindeer calfskin. The leather belt around the hips was tightly filled with four-sided silver brooches whose glittering bosses quavered every time he moved. Outside the upright coat collar he had a large, blood red silk scarf whose corners and soft, thick fringe spread out smartly over the wide breast. His straight, powerful legs were surrounded by shiny black, shorthaired leggings.[1] His entire grand shape meant that ample Finnish blood flowed in his veins, and of the best sort.

Elle, Biettar Oula's buxom wife, whose large, deep blue eyes undoubtedly had to have been smuggled into the race, had, during the pause when the bailiff was writing into the records, forgotten the astutely crafted answers that Biettar Oula today in all haste had supplied her with. She had become infatuated with the young bailiff's bright, oval face, his small, fat hands and the gold braids on his uniform – in this higher revelation of a human being who had five thousand crowns in income and God's countenance almost. Yet – it wasn't just the Sámi's deferential, half timid adulation of a royal Norwegian civil servant. The smuggled-in Germanic blood dared to become sensually hot.

The sharp, vital arches in front of his dimples flowed so alluringly suggestively into the corners of his mouth, while his nostrils arched out with a lust for life.

She was snatched from her ecstasy by little Andi's persistent *Čižži! Čižži!* – He was pulling on his mother's black jacket: *Čižži! Čižži!*[2]

She sat down on the floor, opened her blouse and drew out an almost perilously large breast. The boy snapped and bit firmly into it; he stuck all ten fingers into the breast and cast a contented glance at the bailiff, whose solemn judicial face

---

[1] Made from the hide of a reindeer's lower leg.
[2] *Čižži* is North Sámi for breast.

was crossed by a fleeting smile. In spite of his two and a half years, little Andi had not been able to abandon his old habits.

Every time the door opened, cold gusts in misty gray clouds streamed in over the floor, swept over the platform, sniffed a little at the fat, bald, copper red defense counsel's leg and disappeared. But they again fell down from the ceiling in the form of drops. A tiny, hanging pool aimed at little Andi's mouth – and hit as if it were a shrewd milk mixer. Little Andi happened to express his anger at this in a perhaps somewhat stronger form than he had meant. He said *Bealgalat*: his tongue was still too clumsy to be able to say *Beargalat* which means Devil.

The heat from the red-hot stove gradually melted small, oval holes in the ice on the windowpanes that the little boys outside with possessed impatience fought to get to peak through. They hadn't been as fortunate as Jussa, son of the village's most exceptional Sámi, Jongo. With his winning smile and promise of rides and gold and green forests he had bribed the sheriff's deputy. For safety's sake he also had produced a solemn and sacred lie that he had turned fifteen.

Until now Jussa had kept back. But when he heard little Andi call *Čižži*, he had boldly and quickly crept forward. Such breathless waves went through Elle's large breast.

The bailiff and prosecuting attorney whispered to each other, while the defense counsel sat yawning and grumbled as usual. The sheriff's deputy who was standing with his chest out as if he was Norway's only sheriff's deputy was ordered to fetch Lasse.

The detention door was opened. A couple of shiny wet beads could be seen shimmering in Lasse's watery dull, squinting eyes when the gleam of light from the lamp fell onto him. They involuntarily sought Biettar Oula who had suddenly opened his heavy, strong eyes that now beat down the halfheartedly stubborn servant's last objections.

Lasse walked forward and lay his pitifully thin hands on the bar, stood on one leg and bobbed his knee back and forth so his body swayed. His thick, outturned lips looked like other people's lips that by mistake had been squashed against his arid, pale face. His lower lip hung and pouted in steady homelessness. The worn-out beard hairs were so thin that they reminded one of starving reindeer on an ice-covered pasture. There was something so touchingly sad about his helpless looking face. But now he felt almost happy that Biettar Oula had quelled his last misgivings.

Jussa was a respectful admirer of Biettar Oula. But how he felt sorry for Lasse! He had seen the same helplessly timid expression on several people. This expression that even in good fortune looks doubtfully at fate and dare not really believe its good intention. A tearful warmth went like a shudder through his chest, and he fervently implored God to help Lasse.

— Yes, Lasse had to admit that it was nevertheless he who had been the thief. The decisive word involuntarily supported a sigh of relief from his chest.

Short case. Seven months.

Elle's large chest swelled up and sank again, reassured and strong, so nostrils arched out quivering – as during a long suppressed sigh of love. For God help her if the sheriff's deputy had begun to draw out the answers from her that Biettar Oula had prepared for her, but which now had become a problem for many different reasons. Biettar Oula had threatened them into her with all kinds of plagues and boils, but also with nice words and beautiful promises. Her soul had probably become nauseous and agitated from this whole pack of lies, but everything of no use.

Both Biettar Oula and Elle were spared being put under oath, since their sworn testimony had recently been somewhat shaky. Fortunately! A clammy gust from the false oath's dawning near, but foggy fears had several times today brought cold sweat to Biettar Oula's brow. But his muscles were as strong as sinews, and his nerves were no less stronger. They had persevered in the fight with the writhing, snake-strong ghosts in his soul without giving him away. And with the same strength he slowed down the wildly swinging joy and desire to blab.

But would he have dared to raise his hand when it counted? Hardly. It was only today when Lasse had begun to make trouble that he had had to think of the possibility of having to take an oath. But he had neglected to mention it to Elle who surely would have spoiled everything.

— The spectators streamed out and felt disappointed that the whole thing came down to the triviality that it was just the miserable Lasse who was the thief. But there were also those who suspected the case's real truth, the settled reindeer thieves from the Sámi village's northeastern neighborhood. It's so strange about expert knowledge of a subject.

Nor were the small boys who had heard rumors about many things satisfied with the result. They had waited with great excitement to get to see Biettar Oula – Biettar Oula himself! – led into the jail. But preferably the whole thing should have ended in an appalling tale: with false oath and Biettar Oula's subsequent meeting with the Devil and his whole band. That would have been some sort of story to tell by the dying embers in the fireplace while shadows are on the increase, as the story, titillating and frightening, moves closer to one.

The spectators began to move over the courtyard in order to take the road to the general store that stood out on the riverbank. They walked on their light, soft Sámi shoes as quietly as an owl. And it was therefore all the easier for the sheriff's deputy to draw attention to himself when he made his way through the crowd in a manner appropriate to his office. You see, he was wearing shiny, polished oil-tanned boots that under his choppy gait tore frosty sharp, scraping raucous sounds out of the hard-packed snow.

For the cold was stingingly strong. Bulging, tarry masses of smoke rolled up from the chimneys and shot in strongly accelerating twists right up into the completely still air. Although it was already dark you could still hear axe blows from the firewood forests. The raw, ice-covered birch logs snapped and were split with a splintering crack. You could also hear one or the other muffled sleigh bell rumble in the thick, unpleasant frosty air. A low, thick mist lay over the river that staggered around the level, wood-covered village promontory. The forest ridges on both sides lay comfortably against the low, round-backed, naked mountains.

— The throng from the courtroom had stopped outside the general store. They stood there a while and shivered and alternately knocked one foot against the other. Little by little they filled the general store where there were already some reindeer Sámi at the counter drinking half-pint shots.

"I have a thousand reindeer," boasted Nikko Nille, formerly a good man, now a drunkard and blowhard, one of Biettar Oula's worst enemies, because at one time he had courted the large, pretty, fat Elle with some hope. He bragged. He had six hundred, and they had cost him the humiliation of leading an old, lame widow up to the altar. He had begun to court Elle right after the honeymoon. But when it turned out that it would be a long-term promissory note waiting for the old one's death, Elle thought that after all she would be best served by marrying the most genuine real man she knew even if he besides was the mountain's most dangerous animal.

13

"The entire Hammerfest savings bank is in my pocket," bragged Nikko Nille. A streak of black crust ran over his pale lower lip, and gray foam trickled out of the corners of his mouth.

…"I could buy Biettar Oula's entire herd. But I don't want such reindeer, that –." An involuntary fear prevented him from saying right out what he meant. He started to sing improvised, libelous ditties to Biettar Oula's yoik melody. "Biettar Oula bu-u-u-t-chers winter ni-i-i-ghts." Happy, tipsy men and women joined in, embraced each other and rocked back and forth in step with the melody's rhythms. The reeking, bony faces that barely stuck up from the thick, wooly reindeer coats glistened copper red in a flickering flame of lamplight that in a weak violet tone broke through the humid, liquor-smelling fumes. The beads of sweat became turbid and lead gray from sodden old sweat. The general store itself and all of its contents were fervently included. On the shelves were gaudy materials, kerchiefs and shawls in strong colors: blue and yellow and red in all their resplendent nakedness. In a glass cabinet on the counter was a large selection of brass rings, brooches and various baubles.

The latecomers forced their way in among the drunks and strained with more or less success to look drunk, and in that way the pot or bottle stopped at their mouths too.

"Po-o-or ptar-mi-gan, ptarmigan, ptar-mi-gan. Elle, E-elle, Elle, E-elle!"

But a shock went through the tangled herd when Biettar Oula tore open the door and elbowed his way up to the counter. Little Andi had grabbed hold of his father's long sheath knife. The huge sabre knife with silver-fitted shaft was the boy's solemnly idolized weapon.

Biettar Oula tossed a thick, fat reindeer steak on the counter. "This is to be drunk up in brandy." He was taller and more handsome than the other Sámi, always drank the most expensive liquor, and the merchant always paid him special attention. The pot was put out. He drank a good gulp from it, then passed it to Elle who just took a sip – made a face the way the women do. She took a corner of her silk kerchief and dried herself around her capably sensual mouth, whose red color was heavy with freshness.

Biettar Oula stood silent for a long time, but drank steadily. His black and somewhat pointed eyes that little by little had taken on an ardent luster watched a group that had formed a circle around a loose-mouthed midget that Niiko Nille was getting drunk.

"I wonder how much Lasse's assets will increase while he is gone – ha ha ha! And then he'll be as smart as the Devil alone! Maybe he will even become the sexton in Kautokeino when he becomes so qualified," it drummed out of the midget's head, while a dumb, derisive glance from his wet, blubbering eyes darted a ways up into the air – without coming to rest on anything particular. Nikko Nille laughed demonstratively.

Biettar Oula straightened up. The vein on his right temple swelled up strongly. "Oula! Oula!" implored Elle. He took a couple quick steps over toward the group. The midget got behind the others and screamed with all his might: "He's going to kill me – oh, oh, oh!" But Biettar Oula didn't give a damn about him. However, he grabbed Nikko Nille by the collar, split his reindeer coat in front and in back with a single jerk, right down to the belt, gave him a bear blow on his bare back and then threw him down between a couple of flour sacks so he actually disappeared in a cloud of flour. "Out of the way, damned bastards!" he shouted as he cleared a path through the crowd. He shoved Elle and little Andi out the door and slammed it after himself quite emphatically.

The swarm that had suddenly gotten sober followed them out into the courtyard where their two draft reindeer stood tied to a post eating reindeer lichen.

Elle slipped off her jacket, pulled on a thick, fur coat and then tied little Andi down in the front end of her own sleigh. As supple as an ermine she stole over to the reindeer and slipped the beech saplings that were adorned with yellow, red and blue fringes around the neck of the magnificent, white animal that burned and trembled with the desire to take off. The draw rope was fastened to a crosspiece below the collar.

Biettar Oula had pulled his bearskin collar up over his shoulders and was standing ready to go, with the rein[3] coiled around his right hand.

"You go first!" he said.

Elle gave the rein a little jerk. And when the proud animal took the first powerful, feverish bounds she herself made a few quick, shadowy steps alongside – and

---

[3] Only one rein was used which was fastened to a sort of halter whose one strap went over the forehead, between the eyes and the antlers, the other one over the neck.

then threw herself with a lively leap down into the sleigh. Just as the reindeer was going to cut to the left the rein jumped over her back, and just then the animal changed direction so violently that the sleigh, during the furious swinging, snarled terribly hot-headed and left a white stripe in the dirty, hard-packed snow in the courtyard.

Biettar Oula got his reindeer excited by holding it back a while. The animal danced wide-eyed and pulled in angry greed to be able to stretch its legs with unbound lust. But when he suddenly raised his arms and bent forward for a running start the animal hurled itself off, and Biettar Oula leapt and fell down into the sleigh – like a bird of prey throwing itself on its fleeing victim.

The irresistible speed felt like a fall and tickled his body from the top of his head to his toes. His boisterous, masterly gladdening yoik reverberated through the village, and the mad rush gave the music soul.

The newly so arrogant herd was in an obviously insipid hangover mood, but at the same time close to giving free rein to its hidden admiration for Biettar Oula. This time the midget also got to say the timely word. "Only Biettar Oula could do that."

And Biettar Oula was discussed back and forth with increasing enthusiasm. Hadn't the young, beautiful Norwegian, daughter of the old "wolf" down by the sea last fall followed after him a ways into the mountains but without daring to be seen.

Nikko Nille had had to remain at the general store to get the merchant to sew his reindeer coat together with a couple of sack needle stitches. When he came out – as thanks for the good company – he was met by the midget with the words: "Well, has the smarting in your back gone away?" And the crowd laughed crudely. They nudged the midget and egged him on to continue.

"How many dog barking distances[4] do you think there are between Elle, the mountain's prettiest woman whom you didn't get, and your old, lame, wind-dried scarecrow? I would rather have a sack of tinder-dry reindeer hair as a bedmate than the old one. She's as tough as tanned leather. Not even liquor can finish her off ... Are you perhaps still waiting for her to die? Oh, no, my friend, the old one's

4 *Beanatgullan* (North Sámi) – Dog barking distance: the distance within which a dog can hear, about six miles.

knuckles will not soon tire of holding up her hackneyed body for your eyes! Ugh and ick and damn it!"

The smart aleck's cracked teeth shone yellow in his blubbering jaws with double upper lip, while his evil, runny eyes looked right out into the air.

"Nikko Nille's sweetheart will be an old maid long before the old one dies – ha ha ha."

To tell the truth, Nikko Nille had already picked out a new sweetheart, a young girl, whose superb plumpness was the only characteristic that reminded him of Elle.

"Sing a song about your sweetheart!" the midget began again. But right away the ubiquitous Jussa gave him a blow with flat hand on the blubbering lips. "If you are a coward, do you think you have the right to ridicule people?"

The blow came so unexpectedly that the midget toppled down from his perch. And the crowd poured their laughter on him just as unmercifully as earlier on Nikko Nille.

"Biettar Oula wouldn't take hold of the midget – ha ha ha," someone said with cackling laughter. "He didn't want to soil his hands with that sort – ha ha ha ha."

But the midget had meanwhile hit on a way out. He began to howl and claimed that Jussa had hurt his teeth and lips. The spectators had an excuse to act indignant. Jussa should be beaten. "You should be arrested!" – "You are, God damn me! the worst gypsy child in the entire village!" – "If you are the son of Jongo, do you think, that you therefore have permission to mishandle a miserable wretch?" – "That robber kid who goes and lifts up the jackets of the girls, drives the horses to ruin, and last year was about to ride a bull-calf to death!" – "That he hasn't been jailed long ago! While we have the bailiff here, it's best to set him straight."

The accusations didn't sound new to Jussa's ear, but he nevertheless felt uneasy. His many earlier clashes with the band from the northeast district had scared him. And the midget sometimes was engaged in pure blackmail. And that although Jussa often gave him food and clothing out of the kindness of his heart – without exactly at the moment having fresh misgivings on his conscience. Well, the midget could often go so far as to refuse to accept bribes, but threatened to dish up Jussa's whole register of sins to old Jongo. And Jussa knew all too well that that would be an endless task …

"Beg the midget's pardon," someone said and grabbed Jussa by the hair.

Jussa freed himself, and he and Nikko Nille hurried off. On the way Nikko Nille stopped and said: "It's not easy to go home with a reindeer coat ripped in two."

"You –," Jussa said, "if you have any liquor in the bottle, then I'll run back with it and get the old one to drink herself happy and dead drunk. And then, you know, it'll be easy to steal the keys from her so you can get into the storehouse and change coats.

Then Nikko Nille laughed. "You can damn well drive my reindeer all day tomorrow."

Jussa scurried back with the bottle. Nikko Nille, you see, lodged with old Jongo.

— Nikko Nille took a back road that led west to the riverbank. Here he sat down on a half snowed-in rail fence. The old one had to have time to drink herself drunk.

Here it was quiet and a long way from the village road.

The sky's rim to the north emitted long tongues of northern lights. They quivered in zigzag patterns below the Milky Way's phosphorescent sea, did curlicues and sank twisting to the south. They flew like provoked, legendary serpents that with the deranged force of pain and outright struggling souls writhe on bright embers. Intense reflections fled with spectral speed across the bluish white snow with sparkling crystal dots, quickly moved in a brilliant light over the pine forests on the valley walls and over the pressed flat fog mass on the river. Once in a while this sky's thousand armed, thin, golden white specter opened one or other blue spot with large, calmly quavering stars.

The thin branches of birch and willow trees on the headland on the other side of the river breathed out a thin smell that the cold at the same instant crystallized into white garlands of thick hoarfrost drizzle; the thick-skinned trunks were seen only as black veins. But the bud shells squeezed resin out and hugged the fruit.

A little sparrow whose beak had become tender from the cold and couldn't get the upper hand with an ice-hard bud, sat on a branch with its delicate legs down in the bitter cold, frost drizzle. The cold had snuck in at the tail root and moved so appallingly in over the body. The eyelids flowed together, and the head and neck tried to shrink into the feather covering, but to no avail. The little sparrow fell down into the snow, with its legs pulled up under its stomach … But the last thing it felt was a pleasant wellbeing. It dreamt that it was flying into warm air that was full of sunshine.

— Nikko Nille tightened his eyelids. He looked at a living swarm gliding over a round-backed expanse of snow to the southwest. In spite of the great distance he could see it quite well: for the full moon had just come up in the east …

Biettar Oula doesn't know yet what misfortune is. But it can come. Nikko Nille even said it aloud: "It can come." – Poor Elle! … One pretty day she'll stand there alone, young and helpless. Well! Nikko Nille shouldn't be too hard on her. She'll get a helping hand from him. But when one evening she comes and reminds him of their love in bygone days, then he'll say to her: "Elle, I feel sorry for you. But you know that I love Æira Marit, and she loves me. We are going to have a wedding next month." – Then Elle collapses and cries bitterly. But he says only these words: "Farewell, Elle! May God be with you!" – and says no more, but walks away from her …

Nikko Nille felt cold snow on his back: the merchant hadn't taken much trouble with the seam. Its recent history suddenly contrasted strongly with Nikko Nille's grandiloquent dream …

Good God, will the old one's distended knuckles ever collapse! And still she always threatened that she would "haunt him." As if she hadn't already lived long enough! As if she hadn't already for ten years walked around there as a skin-covered representative from the realm of the dead! And Æira Marit was walking around so young and sweet and plump. – His logical sense snorted in bitter disappointment and had long ago rebelled. He began to drink and drank more and more, became brutal in drunkenness, but to be sure only in the mouth, shrieked and boasted idiotically and wasted his assets. To be sure, it must be admitted that he had begun to steal reindeer. In the beginning he was a chivalrous husband. A husband in the real sense he had probably never been. What was more – he had to this very day maintained his purity. In this respect he could still be said to be a good husband. He was in reality a good head, was a member of the township board. The mayor valued his contributions in a matter. The art of writing though he had never learned. His name was signed in the records with somebody else holding the pen.

How many a spring hadn't he gone with the herd northward with the certain conviction that when he came back again in the fall there would be nothing left of the old one than a little mournful report about her death.

— Nikko Nille plodded homeward.

Jussa and a few other boys were running around in the courtyard teasing the northern lights.[5] Each one held a piece of water-cake up in the air. *Gáhkku! Gáhk-ku!* (Cake! Cake!). The northern lights seemed to become furious and threaten to swoop down on them; but the boys hurried into the smithy and hid.

"Jussa!" Nikko Nille shouted.

"Yes," Jussa said and walked over to him, "The old one is already drunk as a lord and gentle and meek as a warm gut … The keys? – Poof! They will come loose in her hand as easily as the hair on a rotten reindeer hide."

"Can't you go in and get them from her?"

"Ah, – she absolutely wants you to come in and have a drink."

That was too strong an undertow for Nikko Nille. He tried to open the door carefully: but it squeaked alarmingly sharply toward the icy straps on the door panels. Without looking either right or left he stole bashfully over to the old one who was sitting by the fireplace and was lighting tobacco with a pine stick.

"Aah –, are you there, my boy! Now you are really going to get a drink! A drink from old Zare's hand. What? – Do you think perhaps that old Zare would not grudge her boy a drink?" – In her friendly, broadly smiling mouth shone a single, rattling tooth.

Nikko Nille let the brandy really gurgle down through his throat. "And then I have to go into the storehouse."

"Of course, my boy! But first a kiss! … Now, I haven't kissed you since –, damned if I remember whether I've ever kissed you! But now you are going to really give me a banging and noisy one too.

Nikko Nille stood as if unable to speak. The old one had never before hit on this. She would probably not have done it now if Jussa hadn't put her up to it. And

[5] A common boys' game in the mountain villages up there.

she really seemed to want to carry it out. Here "dear!" didn't help, and it was therefore best to grin and bear it … He was already bending down when at the same time he caught sight of Æira Marit who was sitting further up and who was scarlet red with suppressed laughter. But before he had time to move back the old one had already grabbed him by the coat collar. "No, darn if you're going to cheat me out of a kiss this time!"

"Are you crazy, old woman!"

"It makes no difference to you, but a kiss I will have!" – She was breathing heavily from an obsessed ardor after having brought her mouth up to his. During the scuffle she twisted her shorter leg and tumbled down between the posts of the half-finished horse sled Jongo was working on, and immediately the merchant's twine seam burst. There stood Nikko Nille with the left half of his upper body naked, – and the old one was lying between the posts – with her short, crooked leg in the air. Nikko Nille was crouching – suffocating with difficulty breathing, as if he had gotten an ice-cold waterfall over himself. But suddenly he seemed to get an idea. He jerked his knife out of the sheath and rid himself of that part of the garment the kiss-desirous old one was holding in her hand, and ran out.

The round, bowlegged Æira Marit groaned during her ever ready and spurting laughter. Her chubby bosom and stomach so rich in giggles and fat wriggled like a huge flounder below the short jacket, while at the same time she slapped her very fat thighs with her hands. Every so often she had to dry the tears of laughter from her fat cheek bowls, which during the giggling attack had drawn up under her tiny eyes and puckered them together like two narrow-split, tear-trickling fountains on each side of the little, flat nose, which was drawn almost completely into her face.

"Help me up, darn it!" shouted the old one and waved the bottle in one hand and the torn off sleeve in the other.

"Up with you, you old heathen!" said Jussa as he began to pull her. "If you had imagined that Nikko Nille couldn't keep up with the blessed Joseph in steadfast virtue then you were wrong."

The expression of life had excited her to the degree that she flapped across the floor like a lame bird and tumbled down into Æira's lap. "Did you kiss him?" … Look at me, you young goose! … You can rest assured that old Zare probably knows how to live, if for no other reason than to tease you, torture you! … Do you understand? You can go there and stare at each other until you fade away. Like a reindeer cow and a bull who stand each on their own side of a rail fence ... Heh, heh, heh – old Zare also has something to live for, you see!" – And the old one laughed until she was sore and slid down from Æira's short lap.

Æira Marit turned red out of shy modesty, slipped out and hurried up to the storehouse where she lived together with her parents who were also reindeer Sámi. Her sluggish blood had never driven her to expose herself to the hazards of love. And now when Nikko Nille on his part was a practiced ascetic, everything was in the most beautiful order. The outbursts of excitement only made him alarmed afterwards and inexorably condemned to self-denial.

Mearrasámi nissongákti (Sea Sámi women's dress)

II

Highest up on the village headland – where the meadows ended and the birch underbrush began – the winter road turned through a broad, deep drain in the sandbank down onto the ice on the river.

Elle was driving in front.

The reindeer kept an even pace – swayed in a light, lively trot. The road was hard and good; for besides reindeer herders it was used too by people from the village who had outlying fields and firewood on the flat, three-sided promontory along the river.

Biettar Oula sat drowsily downhearted in the sled. Now and then the reindeer nibbled a mouthful of snow and moved their heads on the lookout to both sides. The dark tree roots up under the protruding ridges of snow-covered heather hanging out over the riverbanks sometimes seemed to move over the mist in a rather suspicious way. The reindeer stuck the short stump of a tail apprehensively in the air and made a jerk so Biettar Oula's head was thrown back. At the same moment the misty cold slipped down into the chest of his reindeer coat and iced his blood that was sensitive to the cold from drunkenness and lack of sleep. Shivering, he hurried to pull his head deep into the coat collar in order to make it really cold tight.

Five kilometers above the village they took a side road that led up over a rather narrow, small stream. Thickly frosted birch and willow trees hung outside the low riverbanks, so an almost dark tunnel was formed: you could only see a narrow strip of the sky.

The reindeer's antlers scraped against the branches, and the frost drifted down and covered the face of Biettar Oula who had again fallen asleep. Suddenly he gesticulated wildly and gasped for air. The impressions of reality of his just awakened senses mixed together with evil visions. His fumbling, half open eyes still saw Lasse's head contorted to the rear – far, far up there: he saw it so meaninglessly clearly! He himself sank down into a damp sea of mist, and just as the fall's dreadful source was taking his breath away he was able to scream out …

Elle stopped the reindeer and ran over to him. "Oula! … Ovllážan!" (My dear Ole!) He groaned, held himself at the chest and looked around. "I was just dreaming. – Drive on!"

— Far up in the little, narrow valley the last horse sled tracks swung around a large pile of dry fir trees, while a striped sled end cut at a slant up the eastern valley wall. The reindeer panted energetically up the steep precipice, stretched out, so the belly and muzzle touched the snow, while the tongue hung out of one side of the mouth. The lungs worked like an organ bellows that is stepped on at a rapid tempo, and pumped white streams out of their nostrils.

When the valley wall spread out and flowed over into the naked mountain plateau, Biettar Oula could again breathe widely and freely. The sleds scraped against dwarf birches that didn't even reach up to the snow surface. A couple of ptarmigans flew up, beat with their wing tips a few cross-stripes in the snow, swung in an arc and sank cackling and on outstretched wings down into a willow scrub.

The full moon rose in the east. The sharply outlined shadow of the reindeer sleigh flowed like a narrow, dark blue band over the weakly arching plateau with large and small sweeping waves of light, dry snow dust on old, thin ice crusts that were lying like sparkling shafts over the large, thick snow mass.

From here they could see the village far below to the northeast. Here and there could still be seen spots of light on the houses' shady sides. But they were swallowed one by one.

The plateau was rounded off toward a new valley to the south. Here the snow had been tramped up by reindeer and was full of ski tracks and crossing sled paths.

On the other side of the valley the herd moved, spread out through sparse underbrush, and mowed the frost down from the twisted, squat mountain birches. The snapping crack from the toes of a couple thousand reindeer was heard as a distant, dense sound of pouring rain. The herder, who for a long time was yoiking during the night's monotone stillness, was suddenly heard shouting with a voice hoarse from a bad temper: "Hey, Girje![6] – You damned scoundrel of a dog – will you shut up! Otherwise I'm going to tear your tongue out, you miserable wretch!" – That round, shaggy, tailless dingus that caught hold of a reindeer by staying rather far from the herd, had got its solid animal conscience excited to the degree that in its blind zeal it was chasing the reindeer even though in the middle of the herd. – "Girje!" – The dog yelped a couple more times, but less self-important, and then shuffled to another side without taking notice of the other dogs.

Biettar Oula and Elle drove a little farther on the floor of the valley, along a creek that here and there had stored up fat, yellow gray patches of ice with verdigris edges.

Finally, a little, round clearing opened up in a birch woods sprinkled with a few weather-beaten fir trees. A faint, reddish glow could be seen in the slit in the door of a black, smoky homespun tent whose wooden grating sent crossing, sooty tips up from the smoke hole. A bunch of dogs came wandering out, came to a halt yelping and uncertain – recognized the master and mistress and jumped on them, beside themselves, howling with joy.

"Well – are you here?" said old Mother Biettar as she got up and blew fire into the dying embers. Her long time hired man Aslak also sat upright.

Biettar Oula's unabashed air – and that he had come back at all – released them from asking the painful question, how it had gone. And when Biettar Oula pulled the bottle up from the chest of his coat, the furrows around Aslak's broad mouth bent out into a broad smile rich in lines. With a single breath Aslak conjured up a fresh fire from the embers. He was about to throw tinder wood – a beautiful piece of fat, dry fir root – on the fire, but was stopped by Elle. "You'd think you were a dumb village farmer," she said in a tone that Aslak wasn't used to.

"Yeah," Biettar Oula said, when the bottle had gone around, "Lasse chose the sensible thing, to repent and do penance and be sincere."

Aslak pulled his black, dirty face inside the coat collar, exploded with laughter, threw himself back and laughed unrestrained. "By God, you must let me have

6 A dog name – *Girje* = the motley one.

27

another gulp! … May the Trondhjem seminarian reap much learning and joy from the trip!"

But anyway the topic wouldn't really catch fire.

The pot that was always hanging over the hearth began to bubble on that side where the fire was strongest, and Mother Biettar blew the fat together in the calm corner and poured it up into a wooden bowl. Biettar Oula had a ravenous appetite, cut a large mouthful from a boiling hot piece of meat, dipped it in the fat, chopped it carefully with his strong teeth and let it slide down, while the tears burst out of his eyes: at the same moment he seemed to commend himself to his fate and in self abandonment to await what the heat would do to his stomach.

Mother Biettar asked whether they had been to Jongo. For it was with Biettar Oula's family as with most other Sámi: they wanted to be on good terms with Jongo; it was tied to certain advantages, among others for the reason that Jongo reluctantly bought reindeer from thieving reindeer Sámi.

Yes, they had. They had also gotten little Andi christened last Sunday.

"Did he behave nicely during the christening?" asked Aslak, as he glanced over at little Andi who was already asleep snoring under the fur. "Oh," said Biettar Oula, "he could have been a little better during the ritual, I think. He had gotten away from us while the minister was reading from the prayer book. I found him outside and gave him a real box on the ear. If you don't behave like ordinary people during the christening, I said, then I'll give you another one, you miserable heathen! … But listen to this! That fidgety Nils Snedker goes over to the minister and says that little Andi was baptized at home. He is always sticking his nose into everything. "But you said yesterday that the boy wasn't baptized at home," the minister said and looked at me. "Hm – I said, the minister need not take it amiss," I said. 'I think that Aslak when he christened the boy, he wasn't really into the ritual. And I don't think that I could have it on my conscience if the boy hadn't had a real christening."

"No, – you said that!" said Aslak. "Certainly I read all the ritual's letters. – Even though I never trained as a minister or was Trondhjem educated," he added with a good-natured smile.

"It was a little complicated; but it wasn't so bad all the same!" said Biettar Oula. "For the minister came afterwards and grasped my hand and said that it was done correctly and in a Christian way by me that I wanted to assure that the boy got a proper baptism."

This chat outside the theme of Lasse was like a cat walking around hot porridge. Its congenial tone in contact with liquor had now puffed the modesty out of them. It was with a certain pride – and not just happiness over the successful result, Biettar Oula told about how lithely he had slipped out of the trap. But – he thought – this wasn't the first time either that the sections of the legal traps had passed over him without him getting hooked. It was not for nothing his colleagues had given him the honorary title "the sly one." It happened occasionally that people who had been wronged by being suspected of having killed someone else's reindeer, sought advice from him.

But when Mother Biettar heard that Lasse had begun to make trouble, she broke out in a wild rage and guaranteed him all the world's pain when he came back again. "There is no honor in that scoundrel either! … Let the bastard scrape my intestines! If he so much as tastes the milk of those six cows!" – She waved her arms where she was sitting in the gleam of the fire with the dark brown tent wall as background, and sharpened her glance with brows drawn together around her eyes. – "Beginning to haggle with such a stinking birch bark basket! Haggle with Lasse! … You wouldn't believe you were the son of Mother Biettar! If your father was living, then you would have – hell's bells – gotten a beating!"

"Yeah, but Mother! – What in the hell could I do when –"

"Ah – Talk! … Enough wits you've surely inherited from your father and me that you could have talked circles around the bailiff and the attorney!"

"And swear false! – Are you crazy!" Elle said.

Mother Biettar gasped for air. "If you don't shut up I'm going to box your ear – as much as you know … Good God, so much stupidity I have to listen to! But you, Oula, who are a man, you ought to know enough that you don't demand an oath from the one who is accused … I'm never down in the village; but you may be sure I know more law than all of you!"

Aslak sat as usual with his right hand pulled into his coat scratching himself on the chest. He just sighed and remained silent. Nor did he have anything else to do when Mother Biettar was in that humor. The mountain and the plateaus were hers; anything else was out of the question. Never had anyone ordered her around.

And if one or other innocent reindeer Sámi of a neighbor tried to stand on one's rights, then it always ended that the person concerned had to pack up and leave. Her greatest joy was digging in warm reindeer intestines. She and her son used to drink fresh blood that ran out of the wound of a slaughtered reindeer. And when one winter night or a dark autumn evening they had done away with an unfamiliar reindeer, she was pure fire, got rid of all traces of the slaughtering and incited her son with bold yoiking and devil-may-care words.

Elle, who just as little now as otherwise gave any weight to her mother-in-law's outbursts of fury, sat and warmed herself by the fire; she had spread her coat over her knees. She brooded on her newly conceived feelings. Everything was so oddly strange and new. Her entire life, which had grown together with the mountain and the people here on the plateaus, seemed to her almost like a dream. She felt like a baby bird that has fallen down from a nest up in a tall tree. Yes, now when she was just approaching the tent she thought that she had to take her mother-in-law and Aslak by the hand – as one who has been away a long time … Now the bailiff lies asleep in a white shirt … Under a silk blanket … And it took such a lamentably short time for her to think about what wonders there were up here. Here was the tent. Outside a few sleds with foodstuffs and clothing in them. Yes, then they had a storehouse, surely a well-filled storehouse; but that was down in the village …

Her specialness was contagious. Also Biettar Oula was silent. And Aslak sighed even more.

But into this weakening mood Mother Biettar's strongly felt boasting cut like a fanfare when the herd was heard rumbling like a storm down the valley. "A larger and more beautiful herd than ours does not plow the plateaus around here. It is Mother Biettar who has defended it against thieves and predators, – this herd that flows like living gold slag over the mountains!"

She grasped an old, cast off magic drum that lay discarded under the tent wall and had been saved for "the fun of it." She hit her son on the back with it. "Beat, Oula! You who are dear Biettar's son! – You are now my boy at any rate … Shall we see whether Lasse will come back or not."

Biettar Oula took a hammer of reindeer antler and laid the drum, a large hoop of birch wood, between his knees. On the drum skin, that was stretched over the hoop, various figures had been painted with the pigment of alder bark: a rein-deer Sámi who thrust his skis right into the sun; a *dáža*[7] stood with one leg on a

7 Non-Sámi.

tent and with the other on the devil who on his side clashed with a god and a large fir tree. A wolf stood in front of a church and seemed to consider whether it should go in or not.

"Put this silver ring on the sun!" said Mother Biettar.

Biettar Oula began to beat, first softly, than harder and harder. Mother Biettar intensified her vision and with her hand shaded her eyes from the gleam of the fire. Aslak completely forgot to scratch himself on the chest. His broad mouth contracted into a wrinkled snout, and his large, bristling eyebrows aimed steadily at the ring that finally began to dance on the Norwegian.

"That means death!" said Aslak. "Lasse is going to die." –

"Yeah – damn it all!" said Mother Biettar. "There won't be much of a carcass for the Trondhjem worms to suck on … you're welcome!"

"No, it means that the bailiff intends to come up here," said Elle. She said it quite involuntarily. Biettar Oula himself didn't notice that he was now beating harder – not until he caught himself wanting to beat the whole drum to pieces.

"Let him come then!" he said and hit the hammer shaft right through the skin of the drum that he then threw out the smoke hole. "And if he wants to ransack anything here, then in retaliation I'll ransack the marrow in his knuckles!"

The fire was dying out. In the half dark tent Elle could see the whites in his eyes shining completely around the black pupils.

Oh, no! Biettar Oula certainly didn't think that the bailiff would come on either of those errands …

The big, strong man who had never needed to remind himself of his undivided possession of Elle, succumbed completely to this sudden assault from the ravaging forces of doubt. He who was always used to winning and never had experienced anything like an envy worth mentioning!

When Elle later in the night crept into his reindeer blanket, fearful and whispering beseeching words into his ear, he pinched her on the thigh so that she almost had to let out a shriek. He took hold of one of her nostrils, and it was only by summoning his last self-control that he didn't tear it off.

Sámi almmáibiktasat (Sámi men's wear)

III

It was a whole horse caravan making the 75-mile long trip over the mountain plateau and down to Lafjorden to buy flour and other wares. Jussa was going to go
along for the first time.

*   *

*

— At the light of dawn the caravan went down into an age-old mountain crevice.
Between the ragged cliffs on the steep valley wall stood solitary and remarkably
straight fir trees swaying in the mild west wind that came whistling over the plateau
and sank down into the valley as a light breeze.

Jussa spotted the telegraph. He had to jump down from the sled and kick
one of the poles. It sang, and a heavy metal sound vibrated slowly over the wire up
there. The masonry around the foot of the pole was square; it had been built as if
for show!

— The horses trudged down the sand flecked ice on the river.

The Kvens' houses with blue-painted window molding and doors came into
view and disappeared. The storm had swept the meadows bare and huge snowdrifts piled up along the rail fences. The birch forest's hillsides were so energetically
high. The distant mountain wall's red sandstone shone golden in the winter's first
sunshine and acquired soul from snow stripes and golden gray glaciers in fissures
and furrows.

Jussa's heart swelled from the speed and at the new sights that mixed together with the pleasure of seeing his own young, frisky stallion take the lead. The sound from the sleigh bells that sat high up on a semicircular wooden bow between the shaft ends,[8] had the effect of a work song for the stallion. What a great speed it made. It was as if all its muscles and sinews and joints had been lubricated. The backwind wagged the tail around the loins, and the proud mane fluttered from the bold, bent neck. Dry, light snowflakes came in streams and waves of gusts – like white, foggy clouds.

A pungent smell from the sea broke the tension that the day and a half long trip had stored up in Jussa.

They rode over a small grassy hillside. Up there – right at the edge of a birch forest stood the old wolf's house. Jussa's glance went around in a vision. The large, white-painted farmhouse with porches and shiny brass doorknobs and iron railings along the high, stone steps stood there like a fairytale castle. A globe shone on a pole in the garden. A long row of red-painted storehouses and warehouses led the sight toward the boat landing with its huge hoists and further to the boats in the harbor. And far out there the sea's breakers twinkled toward the heavens – toward the heavens! The waves seemed to float a ways up in the air.

It was as if Jussa suddenly felt crushed. He felt so small. But the stallion lifted his spirit. It was the hero of the moment. Bleary-eyed sea Sámi, slender blond bearded Norwegian fishermen and swarthy Kvens with strong jaws and in sheepskin jackets crowded together around the stallion. As soon as it was unhitched it made a mighty swing, neighed with a vigorous feeling of power and lifted its head high up as it viewed the scene. Its eyes burst out in a burning glance at the sight of a mare. Two strong Kvens grabbed the headgear; but they had to, although kicking against, walk with …

It really seemed as if Jussa got his share of the attention too. His snow white jacket of reindeer calfskin and the new otter skin cap with a large, four-sided crown of black cloth, the white, neat Sámi shoes and not least his coal black eyes, which the speed and the new impressions had given a warm radiance, awakened a certain curiosity. There was even a young, pretty girl standing and looking at him behind the curtain in the large, white-painted house.

---

[8] Russian harness. The bow stretches the reins between the hames and shafts right out to the sides.

"Here comes the wolf!" – Be careful, he doesn't bite your head off!" said one of those standing around. Old Norum came ambling down from the warehouse, stopped and, to get some shade, put his hand against his leather cap, whose threadbare lapel was folded down in front. He began again to walk stiffly with short, rapid steps when his strongly leaning upper body was about to bring him out of balance, and his legs also would bend way too much at the knees. The red and remarkably small grizzled whiskers contrasted with his snow-white and still very thick hair. His face was hale and ruddy – for being the face of a man almost eighty. His coat he had pulled over his shoulders; but a thick, red woolen scarf covered the rest.

Jussa felt uneasy. The gruff name had made him charming. And at home he was used to seeing a hostile assailant in just about every other person. – But when the old man's face was touched by a heartfelt and seductively beautiful smile, Jussa became completely warm in his heart.

"What kind of a brave, little fellow are you?" the old one asked in Sámi.

"I am the son of Jongo," Jussa replied. His voice betrayed him: he had to swallow the words. He was addicted to this mixture of fear and a feeling of gratitude toward the old one.

"So, – you are the son of my old customer, Jongo. Yes, I could almost sense that … And then what a fine horse you have. Has old Borken perhaps been cast off now? – For this one has not been here before."

Jussa had never in his life seen such a kind-hearted and nice man.

"I'll tell the farm hand to take good care of your horse. And you will have a bed in the main house." – And as he shuffled on he said once more: "So, you are the son of Jongo."

Jussa blushed with joy and pride at having gotten such an honor.

Although old Norum was already out of the picture – the business had long since been taken over by one of his sons, he went there anyways and gave orders – out of old habit. He couldn't stand the thought that he no longer could be useful. He had an inexhaustible abundance of advice and orders that his children and people had to listen to – and sometimes they too had to pretend that it was of importance to get advice and tips from "he himself."

Groaning, he was climbing the steps to the farmhouse when he caught sight of the cook throwing out rinse water right beside the kitchen door.

"Jolline!"

The girl looked up frightened.

"Come here!" – His old, round back straightened up. – "You yellow swine! I'll teach you to mess up my courtyard! – You fat-bellied mare! If I were to do what was right I would stick you in the toilet pail and wash you off out by the horse manure pile behind the stall. Don't just stand there and stare at me with your round cow eyes!"

He turned toward a couple fishermen who were standing nearby and laughing courteously. "Gentlemen, do you know why she is called Jolline? – Her father, the Læstadian preacher, has explained the riddle to me. 'She was conceived out in a jolly boat,' were the preacher's words to me."

This little rebellion of the soul awakened a new restlessness in him. He shuffled down to the general store with such short, rapid steps as if he had a sack of flour on his back and was about to stumble. The clerk had to fill his purse with small change. His position demanded that he have coins to give away. He was in the habit of suddenly engaging one or two men to do this or that – blast away a rock knoll – God knows what for! – or to repair an old, cast off boat. In the evening he called together "the work people" to "settle," a transaction that he always carried out with solemn enjoyment.

So strong was his passion for a work force that some twenty years back he began to realize that "the upstarts" had made life difficult for him, so he drove with full speed ahead into bankruptcy anyway. That way the business came into the hands of his son.

No wonder therefore that he considered the upstarts as cannibals, "who were bred in sorrow and envy." In the old days when in the literal meaning he was the district's father, there wasn't such a deluge of "these badly scored mugs, who always seemed to grimace at the smell of their own evil," – "And then there were still houses in Finnmark that could summarily settle and with dignity receive bigwigs, – even if it was a royal guest. And we young gentlemen stayed with the great families in Bergen and England and Holland and Russia and learned courtly mannerisms.

*   *

*

Hardly had Jussa gotten food into himself before he hurried down to the shore. He stared down into the gray-green water and saw so many strange things down on the bottom. It wasn't flowing, this water, nor was it still; it just rocked, sighed slowly and was so heavy and playfully strong as it rolled rocks onto the shore. He saw the edge of the sea bump right against the sky. From the deep sea mass around the earth the motion of the sea drew its strength and powerful mass here by the shore: it was like somnolent expressions of life in the paw of an inconceivably large, sleeping animal.

He inspected the boats. They were fitted with iron. And then there were anchors and chains and masts as thick as tree trunks. People who were masters of such, had to be big … He was again gripped by despondency and felt homesick.

— A young girl came riding down to the shore, right toward him, and braked with her legs so Jussa got to see her well-formed calves. And when she had gotten up he was absolutely certain that it couldn't be anyone else but Elna, daughter of old Norum. She had on a white cap and white gloves that reached up to her elbows, an attractive blue coat and galoshes with leather-covered legs. She stood right opposite the setting sun that cast golden streaks on her light golden hair and made the warm, soft radiance of dew in her brown eyes more distant.

She looked at him for a moment.

"Are you from the mountains?" she asked in Sámi and smiled friendly.

"Yes."

"I would really like to have Sámi boots like you have on. Can you get me a pair?"

Yes, he could. – What did they cost? – They wouldn't cost anything. But he blushed right away. He had caught himself being forward: it was dumb, not permissible of him to offer her Sámi boots free. What did she care about getting a present from him? – And he blushed even more.

No, it wasn't possible: he would rather pay for them, he said – pretended that she didn't notice his embarrassment.

"Tell me, do you know Biettar Oula?" she asked.

Yes, Jussa did. He couldn't prevent himself from taking an inquiring look at her. Now it was her turn to blush ... "No, I ask only, because I think you resemble him."`

Jussa swelled up, and his face and attitude immediately took on an uplifting character. He had a lot to tell about Biettar Oula, and she had the courage to admit her interest in this "dark, strong man." – "Do you think he can cast spells? – I don't know. But he is like the land up there. He is so unbounded. My teacher also says that, the telegrapher. You perhaps don't understand what I mean. I mean that he sort of has no boundaries, especially when he stands quite still and looks at one. My teacher says that she could feel like running away with him ... It must be horribly strange up there – behind the plateau ... And then there is an endless plateau behind your village. – Yes, isn't that so? I have such an incomprehensible urge to travel up there, although I'm almost too afraid ... I think Biettar Oula bewitches a woods if he just walks through it."

And then she said in self-denying abandonment: "He is so exceedingly strange, Biettar Oula!" – The look in her brown eyes suddenly took on a heaviness that had a crushing weight, – at the same time as it pulled her quite close to him. But he only barely grazed her in her elevated closeness; for suddenly she wrapped herself in her ladylike everyday look which like a magic cloak made her more distant from him. She felt obviously embarrassed for having exposed herself so much.

"You can go through the kitchen, then you'll get coffee and pastry from the girl," she said as she walked up.

She had her father's smile; but it was hallowed in a young girl's soul and explained through a young girl's face.

Jussa looked at the sea and felt Elna's glance in it. He blinked with his eyelids and felt squeezed by a strange malady ... Then finally he managed a sigh of relief. What was it? – He was almost afraid.

— On the shore on the outer side of the fjord bottom the sea Sámis' turf huts could be seen as black, smoky dots between dirty footpaths over the snowdrifts. A couple sea Sámi came rowing along the ice at the bottom of the fjord and docked at the dock. Such dirty and poverty-stricken looking people Jussa hadn't seen before. The homespun coats were yellow brown from cod-liver oil, and the scarfs were stiff from glistening filth.

— Jussa walked into the kitchen. He stopped a while at the door and then sat down on a bench. At home he had been in the minister's, sheriff's and merchant's kitchens. So he knew how to behave. But here it was so impressively large and splendid altogether. The base cabinet had eight doors. The cabinet in the minister's kitchen at home had no more than four.

The girl served him coffee and pastry. Elna had asked her to do it, she said.

While he sat and ate, he heard the gray wolf sneeze quite violently in the dining room and afterwards clear his throat and groan entirely happy. And when the gray wolf opened the door Jussa bent back to look in and got to see about as much as he had seen of the minister's kitchen at home.

"You eat like a little nobleman," said the gray wolf with his good-natured smile. Yes, thought Jussa, this isn't the first time either that I am eating in the big shot's kitchen.

"Jolline, you would probably like to go to a prayer meeting this evening. You toil away so much the whole day that you need to get out a little."

That didn't surprise Jolline. After the hurricane in the morning she was ready to get a little extra attention.

The gray wolf asked Jussa to come along into the living room. But then Jussa no longer felt equal to the situation. How he was going manage in there was beyond his understanding. He stopped in the dining room and was on the verge of asking to get out of going further in. "No, come in!" said the gray wolf and nudged him in between the heavy drapes.

The light from the large and elegant chandelier flowed out as if from a marvelous light source; the flame could not be seen. And the colors on the table and chairs and everywhere streamed into each other, without Jussa being able to figure out which colors they were: it was either red or yellow or blue. But here and there it shone of gold and silver and copper. The walls were as if non-existent: Jussa barely suspected them. And in a room inside he saw an even greater glory flowing together.

The minister's small boys who were visiting Elna ran around the chairs and played at the top of their lungs. The little, fat angels in tricot made noises and talked and stampeded – without a trace of respect for the sanctuary they were in

– didn't even become scared when the gray wolf hushed them. And then it was so funny to hear children speaking Norwegian!

Jussa found himself sitting at the table. He touched the tablecloth; it was like touching a filly's back. While the gray wolf rested in front of a large glass cabinet and groaned and sought to find "the little box," that he wanted to show Jussa, Elna had taken out a whole bunch of pictures and many strange things that Jussa's eyes and thoughts however weren't able to notice. She was so close to him: he felt her breath. In the shadow of his large, black forelock his dewy eyes sought Elna's boldly growing bosom that arched over her one forearm that she supported against the table edge. – And she was still only a child yet! … He was almost stupefied by the sight … Jussa had seen women before, beautiful, fair, tall women; but their bodies had been so far inside the strange garments that his thoughts could hardly reach them: the lines on the many pads and skirts completely threw someone off. He had hardly enough tied anything femininely human with a lady. But all distant, weak dream images suddenly were kneaded together and sprang forth in Elna's young body. The simple, loose blouse swelled so earthly solid and alive in two places. The dress lay around her hips, and the reddening gleam on her bare, white neck carried a message from the sentient warm blood … But it was the woman in the gleam of transfiguration that had here stepped forth for him. Fair and self-assured and tall – in clothing that became her like loving thoughts. The bow alone around the braid was like a leaf of a beautiful flower! But most beautiful of all was the smile and the charming subconscious friendliness that shone out from her oval, pure-lined face …

*   *

*

The day's gentle winds were followed later in the evening by a roaring storm that stripped thick chunks of ice off the frigid sea and dashed them against the rocky knolls on the shore.

— The large Kven cottage with a low ceiling and small windowpanes was absolutely crowded.

Everyone had taken their places, and their silence was somber. They were filled by a tickling anxiety of the enjoyment of fear that was now going to be revealed to them; for it was Brother Karjalainen from Finland who was going to preach this evening.

Karjalainen got up, thin and dark and tall. He climbed up like a revelation of the feeble gleam of light that the lamp cast out into the steam-filled air in the room. The immensely strong look from his black eyes glided slowly over the gathering and was felt by everyone as the calm heavy pressure before bad weather. He folded his hands and closed his eyes; his chest worked hard. Then he began quite unobtrusively and said: *"Isä meidän, joka olet taivaissa!"* (Our father, you who art in the heavens!).

The words were heard as distant ocean ripples. The syllables resounded, sighed – and crashed into each other slowly with a booming sound in that he prayed with demented sincerity, in helpless devotion, in dispirited humility. And then when with a mysteriously mournful soft increase in pitch, that trembling hung in his quivering heart, he beseeched God in the fifth prayer: *"Ja anna meille meidän velkomme anteeksi!"* (And forgive us our trespasses!), then the women broke into sobs, – without the pain of dismay, merely dissolved in a vague ecstasy. The swells in Karjalainen's powerful soul in his huge body transmitted out over and through the listeners, rendered them impotent, poured ticklingly cold and hot over their nerves.

Karjalainen sat down. He began singing a hymn, others in tune chimed in, and the song ascended. A cold chill of voluptuous shaking hurled it into tremors, and the air in the house vibrated as if it were full of living blood, hunting in sensual anxiety and unease.

Frightful were the words, which as if in distress twisted up from Karjalainen's chest when he began to speak. Poverty-stricken sea Sámi in dirty yellow homespun clothing and with naive, fearful expressions on their broad, bony faces rocked with their upper bodies and stared helplessly around. Fanatically wide eyes from Finland's dark forests and the women's wailing bewitched the Norwegian fishermen, calm and light until now. Above this chorus of smoldering sighs and cries of groaning that little by little increased to a cry of distress in unison, Karjalainen's euphoniously resonant voice hovered, while the storm from the Arctic Ocean every so often made a violent spurt, howled against the house corners, bellowed loudly up through the valley and bombarded the large, desolate plateaus. People shrieked and clung to each other. Karjalainen stopped and stood as a god and watched the human maggots writhe in the dust.

But some were hideous in their untimely, feigned ecstasy, for example a woman from Jussa's home village. She was the first one to leap up and bellow with an unseemly broad mouth.

Then Karjalainen again raised his voice. His face began to clarify. With an intoxicating joy and inflection that was moist from an overwhelmed heart he reads aloud from the thick bible: "For the lamb who is in the middle of the throne shall watch over them and lead them to the fountain of life, and God shall dry every tear in their eyes." – He smiled, he laughed, the audience smiled, laughed, actually broke into laughter. Some leaped up, jumped and danced in the really and truly devoted joy of madness, overturned chairs and benches and stools, threw themselves blissfully howling into each other's arms, women and men in one whole lot. A fat, young woman flailed like a Halling man. Her pants slid down over her knees. Her husband jerked her in the jacket: "You, – pull your pants up!" But she noticed nothing. The leaders sent each other a shining smile. "David also danced naked before the Lord's ark."

And as the dancers little by little became weary and lay stupefied as after an ecstasy, the place's village elder got up and said: "Let us confess our sins!"

The fat woman suddenly awoke, grabbed hold of her pants quickly, pulled them up and dished up a single sin committed – a traveling brother – and when one is traveling a long way and even a faithful brother, then it isn't always so easy –, and she received absolution with a broad smile. The bellowing woman from Jussa's home village wouldn't stand back and related a nauseating story.

And since the many oppressed consciences were lightened, so that one for the moment could be said to be well-nigh without sin, the mood began to climb. The men cut tobacco into pipes, talked about horses and chatted about Our Lord. The women camped around Karjalainen, and each outdid the other in sweetness and abundance of stories about the spirit's almost unbelievably marvelous good deeds toward them. The eaters gorged on cured meat and salmon and imbibed one cup of coffee after the other.

*   *

*

Jussa was overwhelmed when late in the evening he walked home along the shore by the bottom of the fjord. Karjalainen was great and noble as a prophet when he asked, when he sang, when he spoke and when he sat completely silent … *"Isä meidän, joka olet taivaissa!"* – The syllables still lurched in his ears, heavy booming and slow like the waves that in the abating weather rumbled in lazy, sleepy blows in over the fjord … If he could sometime speak like Karjalainen! Yes, if he could become a minister … Stand under the church's high arch, high up in the pulpit, alone, isolated from the multitudes, in long, black kirtle and with a white collar around his neck, – pallid and praying, while everyone's eyes rested on him.

— He stopped at the garden fence. There was light in only one window, and it was high up. Above the jalousie he saw a shadow move a couple times under the white-painted attic ceiling. A pleasant feeling followed with the thought that Elna was now going to bed and closing her eyes, her brown eyes, whose glance had such a wonderful weight. It became more and more pleasant to think about, while he was standing there. And he stood there a long time. His eyelids began to slide shut; finally he saw only a shimmering speck of the radiance that the Northern Lights conjured from the large, shining globe in the sea. He could still hear the calm breakers' drifting movement down on the beach.

And when his head sank down in the wooly coat sleeve he dreamt that her spirit warmed his face, and that the veiled glance from her brown eyes was slowly sliding toward him … He awakened just at that moment when he was going to grab her glance with his hand.

Sámi goahti (turf hut)

IV

One hot summer day Biettar Oula sat in the shade of one of the gray wolf's Nordland boats down on the shore and ate dried reindeer meat to strengthen himself for the long march into the mountains. He had bought a whole reindeer load of coffee and sugar and a few necessary small things – such as sewing needles and thread spools and balls of yarn, a small kettle and a little soap. Elle had gotten even finer at that recently.

When he was ready, he stuck the rest down in a ptarmigan bag of tanned reindeer hide, which he tied to the packsaddle, and was about to take off when the gray wolf came shuffling down, hurrying fast and heavy in his steps.

The gray wolf, when he caught sight of Biettar Oula this morning, had sworn a juicy oath that he was going to rake him over the coals so that he would smell burned. But he had put it off and put it off and meanwhile had wandered around in the courtyard and through the rooms and vented his spleen on his own people: he didn't have to think about it. No, if it had only been last year! Then the story was so fresh, and then he would have sent twenty balls of rusted iron through Biettar Oula – the damned badger scoundrel … Ach! We get old, and age abrades our passions, our courage. Only a half score of years ago the gray wolf didn't feel any doubts when it was a matter of easing a nagging anger or an unsaid truth. But now! He had even hit on excusing compliancy. A sensible person like Biettar Oula – he had thought and said today – would of course have chased the quixotic girl home, if he had caught sight of her, – and the whole story was of course a year old now. He couldn't help it that the girl had thought up something so crazy as to begin to follow after him into the mountains …

49

Nor was there now any elevating compassion with the gray wolf who steered his course toward Biettar Oula, but just a weak hope that the bold wrath would show up at the decisive moment; it was, in any case, worth an attempt. He stopped and shaded his eyes with his hand ... Perhaps it was best anyways to begin carefully. "Isn't it Biettar Oula?"

Yes, it was.

"You have your herd in the mountains to the west?"

"Yeah, some twenty miles from here."

"Isn't it hard to walk around dressed so warmly in this heat?" – Biettar Oula had two homespun jackets on, and the large, four-sided crown of his cap was filled with eider down. But there wasn't a drop of sweat on his sunburned, completely brown face; the muscles on his well-formed limbs were firm and strong as sinews.

"Yes, yes, good luck on the way back then!"

The gray wolf had worn himself out today to implement his big decision, – and then nothing came of it! He sat down on a log and sat quietly for a long time sad and dog-tired. Finally, the old fighter, the once so brave and autocratic gray wolf, broke into tears. He hadn't believed that it was so completely past for him. God help him! – He couldn't even bring himself to hamstring a mountain Sámi! ... It was, as he only now became aware of, that the backs of his hands had begun to turn black and had round hollows with thin, shiny membranes and grainy folds after the disappeared fat padding. He had during the past few years often spoken about taking a trip to his old friend Consul Kakowstzeff in Archangel. This year because of poor health he had to postpone until next year. "And Lord knows whether anything will come of the trip too!"

And the old man cried so painfully. The anxiety-filled feeling of wasting away to nothing had come so brutally over him.

*   *

*

Biettar Oula had come out of the deciduous forest. His old, familiar path climbed steeply to the mountains, along a gray, moss-grown, rock-strewn slope where old crumbled bones shone in the sun, pale and partly coated with thin turf. – The remains of one of the numerous Russian bandit hordes, Karelians from northern Russia who in the old days were engaged in plunder and murder among the Sámi.

Up here on the mountain a group of them one dark autumn evening got hold of a mountain Sámi and forced him to be a pathfinder. The descent was difficult, said the Sámi, and they therefore had to tie themselves firmly to each other. He himself went in front with a torch in hand and quite fast; he jogged. But when he had come right out onto the edge of a precipice he threw the torch out over the mountain and himself ducked down behind a rock, while the Karelians ran after the torch, tumbled down and killed themselves.

— Biettar Oula had come far into the mountains and was walking in the summer night's cool sunshine. Here and there was a spot of grass that year-old, shriveled-up plants gave a grizzled appearance. Yellowish gray-green reindeer lichen crept densely and thick up over the rock-strewn slopes at the foot of the plateau's eternally snow-covered top. A brook rippled between gray, shaggy willow bushes and tangled, creeping dwarf birch with round, nail-sized leaves and disappeared into a cloudberry bog.

A plover flew up from a gray flat stone, chattered with its long, sad bowing-down beak a sickening, melancholy sound, full of the plateau's solitude – and sank slowly with careful, dispirited wing beats onto another gray flat stone.

There was a golden gleam over the close peaks' snow, and the distant peaks bathed like white swans in the night's radiance. And the pure color of heaven was deep as an ocean.

Sometimes a distant, subdued sound of running water on scree slopes and crevices cut into the plateau's high-born stillness.

— Biettar Oula walked into a wavy crevice and suddenly a large hollow opened up with a little, long and narrow lake on the bottom. Right down by the shore stood his summer canvas tent. A thin, blue smoke climbed up from a small bonfire outside the tent. On the glacier in the background lay the reindeer sunning themselves, at a most delightful peace from the mosquitos. Further down on a dry tuft of moss lay Aslak with staff in hand and the dogs around him.

"Áčči! Áčči!" (Father! Father!) shouted little Andi who had been practicing throwing a lasso onto a willow bush. Elle was sitting at the fire and sewing white homespun pants for Biettar Oula.

"Welcome back, Ovllážan! – Well, how was it on your trip?"

"Yeah – thanks! Just fine."

He had a lot to tell, while he sat and ate boiled, fresh trout, and Elle examined the things bought. He had reports all the way from the inland village. Jussa had traveled to a large city in Finland to train for the ministry. "He will no doubt become a gentleman," Elle said. "And a believer he can also become when he has studied God's word so much. And then he was so good in Finnish."

And Nikko Nille's old woman is supposed to be sick, Biettar Oula reported.

"No – is that so! Well, then Nikko Nille is bursting with impatience after getting the death message … If she doesn't perk up or start walking again."

"I could," said Biettar Oula, "be tempted to send him a special delivery with the news if he was a little closer. The news is so valuable that I could buy his friendship part and parcel for that. He could maybe even give up his sly idea of moving in front of us southward in the fall and snatching those reindeer that disappear from us during the migration. He has become long-fingered, Nikko Nille."

Biettar Oula was given to getting indignant on behalf of morality when a decent man succumbed to temptation. And now it was, besides, the light summer; his mind was so light and bright, and his misdeeds almost a year old: Biettar Oula only slaughtered in the fall or in the winter; then the meat and hides were best … So Biettar Oula could well talk about long-fingered men now in the summer when the mind was light and easy.

Elle laid her arm over his shoulder, looked quite modestly down and said: "If you could only discard your wild habits, Ovllážan!"

Biettar Oula smiled; he usually brushed her aside with a smile, when she attempted to speak about his "wild habits." Stronger words she couldn't well dare to use. But the subdued expression made her so remarkably modest – and irresistible. Biettar Oula stroked her down her lovely, plump back. No other woman in the mountain had such big, buxom limbs. Her bosom swelled under the short, loose jacket.

— "Look!" said Biettar Oula. "Just look! … See what dexterity he has! He tightens the lasso just at the right moment. The lasso chokes the bush like a weasel.

Just look! … The bush lashes and struggles against like a calf … People may be right, that Andi will become the mountain's first man."

"But where is the mountain's first girl?" asked Elle and glanced with a half roguish, half modest smile at him.

"Oh, don't be so angry at that! You are real young still."

"But remember that Andi was three last Midsummer Day … And I am still in my best health. It would be excellent to have a villager as a son-in-law, you know. We could then live with our own son-in-law when we're down in the village during the winter. And Biettar Oula's daughter would surely attract the village's best suitors. … A daughter-in-law of a village girl you don't want, I suppose?"

"A village girl as daughter-in-law!" – Just the thought of that was for Biettar Oula an abomination: What mountain Sámi would go there and get married to a village girl? – "She would soil our tent with cow barn smell … It would strain us to have a cow girl sitting on a bench in the tent – for she will naturally want to have a bench. And the devil would take care of her so that one fine day she wouldn't fall down in the fire and burn up in front of us! – For you can't mean that Biettar Oula's son would start to clean up the manure and cut hay for a couple dirty cows!"

— They sat and looked at the reindeer that lay in small groups on the glacier. Their ears fluttered in comfort, their eyes squinted in the early morning sunshine, and their jaws moved softly during the cud chewing.

Little by little the animals arose, limbered up with a couple stretches of the body and walked down from the glacier. At the same instant the dogs sounded the alarm; but Aslak just reeled off the usual words of abuse, turned onto his other side and slept on. The reindeer were beginning to be concerned with forming the new stubs of antlers that were still filled with blood and cartilage covered with hairy skin, – banged and hammered them with their hoofs on the one back foot or against a rock and twisted their eyes up so as to inspect the shape.

— Mother Biettar who was lying in the tent sleeping, stuck her head out of the tent opening. "Good morning, Oula! – You've come back. We'll have to milk the cows soon!"

When the sun stood right in the east, people rested, and the reindeer spread out grazing over the range of hills.

In Schatten

Gáibideamen vearu sápmelaččain
(Tax collecting from the Sámi)

V

Nikko Nille had sure enough thought of arranging it so that he would be at a suitable distance in front of Biettar Oula during the migration southward.

But while he and the other mountain Sámi pored over the plans and did some spying, Biettar Oula one beautiful day had packed up and had taken off, before anyone knew about it.

— He had taken the autumn quarter on the north side of the inland valley, some thirty miles above the village, just there where the pine forest ended and the mountain birch began, by a brook and just below the mail carrier's footpath.

Biettar Oula was not the man who avoided the main road and sought out-of-the-way places – in the manner of reindeer thieves.

There was sleet now during the days, and the trees around the tent were hung with wet clothing. – One afternoon Nikko Nille stopped outside the tent and said *Buorre beaivi*! (Good morning).

"*Ipmel atti!*" (May God grant) answered Biettar Oula, received him warmly and led him into the tent.

"Some of your reindeer have gotten lost during the migration," said Biettar Oula, while they sat down on the reindeer hides.

"Yes, that's right. And now I'm traveling through the neighboring reindeer camps to look for them."

"I see that there is one of your reindeer in our herd."

Nikko Nille's astonishment was so immediate and, for the moment, so little concealed, that Biettar Oula would have become alarmed if he had seen his wide-eyed expression.

For, frankly speaking, Nikko Nille didn't see much hope that a stray reindeer that had gotten within Biettar Oula's reach would see the light of day again.

But Biettar Oula kept an ordinary, sincere face, – as if he were used to speaking about stray reindeer that were in his herd.

For if one could make amends a little for his in certain respects bad name with a single miserable reindeer, then Biettar Oula could gladly assume the bother of letting his lasso remain untouched over his shoulder. And Elle smiled quite delighted and was almost equally as surprised as Nikko Nille. A favor here, a favor there! – And the plan was approved by Mother Biettar. To be sure she had said, to begin with, that it was a damned untimely sacrifice at the altar of respectability; when she thought about it, then it seemed to her that a little good reputation would be nice to have too. "Yeah, yeah! Let the animal go then!" she had said.

— Talking about looking for stray reindeer was actually only a pretext of Nikko Nille to be able to pay Biettar Oula a thank-you and reconciliation visit. It was of course Biettar Oula who had first brought the very promising message to the mountains about the old one's sickness. Later it had wandered days and weeks over the large stretches, came to Nikko Nille, and one fine day it came back to him, but this time in the shape of a death message. And Nikko Nille blushed when he was told this.

So he had more than gladly granted Biettar Oula the pleasure of doing away with one of his reindeer. What did a reindeer more or less have to say now, when he was drunk with vague sweet inklings of the time of Advent: all his inexperienced dreams and longings beckoned the wedding.

Nikko Nille beamed with happiness and modesty where he sat and enjoyed Elle's and Biettar Oula's profuse hospitality.

Elle changed the sedge grass[9] in his soft Sámi boots[10] and it was so infinitely nice to speak openly and friendly with her. He had gained Biettar Oula's friendship. And when the chips were down it was good to have the reindeer intact. Now one of these days he was going down to the village – together with his sweetheart, yes together with his sweetheart! He confided that to Elle and Biettar Oula then in strict confidence.

Good grief, how he wished them all the best!

He was ashamed to display his overwhelming abundance of happy feelings; now he was able to let them keep the feeling of being something special.

"Æira Marit is the best match in our parish too," said Elle.

"Nor with you can any bachelor match up," said Biettar Oula. "You are legally trained and are part of conducting the parish's business."

Yes, Nikko Nille wished them all the best! He did that deep in his heart.

— But when Biettar Oula later accompanied him to the herd, it was nevertheless that the sight of it formed a small, suffocating clump in Nikko Nille's chest.

It didn't take long before they caught sight of Nikko Nille's reindeer. The one ear tip had been clipped right off, and the other ear had an angle cut on the outer edge.

Hesitating, Nikko Nille held onto the tar-stiff lasso hanging over his right shoulder and going under his left arm. But when Biettar Oula didn't make a sign that he wanted to catch the reindeer Nikko Nille had to take his lasso off. He wound up a slip noose extending long in a suitably small ring, snuck closer to the reindeer and cast, but missed, – was dumbfounded and nervous and miscast yet another time.

Then Biettar Oula took the lasso, wound it up to the last fragment and cast, so that it sang and whistled into the bone loop, – and there dangled the reindeer

9 Carex vesicaria.
10 Summer shoes: bottom of smooth sealskin. The upper part and leg of stripped reindeer skin.

far inside the herd, as if it had gotten a harpoon in itself. He pulled it to himself without moving from the spot.

Nikko Nille again felt a small knot in his chest. But he was moved and overcome when Biettar Oula himself uttered a wish to be invited to the wedding; there would sure enough be a gift that no one else had gotten yet.

Biettar Oula really set store by being a friend of Nikko Nille!

Nikko Nille wished him all the best!

Sámi *lávvu* (summer tent)

VI

Nikko Nille had left a while ago, and the twilight had already set in.

A large, crackling fire was burning outside the tent. Mother Biettar sat and pounded sedge grass with a thick birch club. "The anvil" consisted of a thick, flat stone. Biettar Oula was busy carving a spoon from reindeer antler with rosettes and zigzag lines. Elle spread out the pounded sedge grass bundles on a few flat stones to dry.

Now and then Biettar Oula let his glance roam the surrounding grove – out of old habit.

Suddenly the dogs raise a racket. He hushes them. He hears rotten branches snap and there's a rustling in fallen leaves. Between the tree trunks three people are glimpsed coming down the postal road. They swing down to the fire. Biettar Oula immediately recognizes two of them, the postal carriers; but the third one?

"Yeah – darn! – Isn't it Lasse!" said Aslak and completely forgot to call him the Trondhjem seminarian.

Lasse was in a black hat – and pale as the most learned devil, had a belt around his waist – like a pious preacher – and not around the hips as people of doubtful virtue usually have, had short-clipped hair and took off his hat when he greeted the master and mistress. He was on the whole what the gray wolf would call "an amiable person with courtly mannerisms."

Biettar as well as the others were unpleasantly impressed by Lasse's arrival; besides they hadn't really expected him yet. Sure, Biettar Oula had taken a dreadful oath from him that he would never betray the secret, but in any case …

Still they gave Lasse all possible attention. Biettar Oula let it be apparent – for the sake of the postal people – that he didn't have a score to settle with Lasse: he dared to be jokingly sarcastic towards him; but the words seemed to sting himself most.

Lasse often used Norwegian words and phrases; he had made a "stool" and tied a "net," made a "steel basket" and learned "nice writing."

The postal folks decided to spend the night here. It was still about twenty miles down to the summer dairies where they had a riverboat to row down to the village.

The postal folks told the news from the big world, while they sat and ate.

"The bailiff in Vadsø," one of them related, "had a meeting with the bailiff in Hammerfest. It was a matter of the articles of the law that they were not in agreement on, and it is supposed to have gotten hot between them. They both know their paragraphs; yeah, the bailiff in Vadsø is supposed to be the best anyways."

"Yeah – but he's nothing against attorney Lunda!" said Aslak. "What a fellow; he's sly and learned, he is! Yeah, there is no paragraph that he can't and doesn't know how to find fault with … But then he is good and expensive too!"

— Biettar Oula said that Nikko Nille had been there this afternoon. But what amusement the postal folks could get from Nikko Nille wanting to travel with his sweetheart down to the village, none of the others could understand. It was probably so that something irrevocably laughable had begun to stick to Nikko Nille, but anyway … Could it be that the old one had come back to haunt them? – Although, yes, it was definitely not impossible that she did just that …

— Much was discussed; but sometimes they were silent, stared at the fire and thought about what they had spoken about.

The red flames flickered and licked the fat smoke that was so black the cloudy, night-black sky paled against its long, uneasily swimming neck. A push from the wind every so often bent the tongues of flame into broad, rippling wave blades that at the next moment again stretched into the air, made themselves thin and long, flitted ready to fly, loosened, but were suddenly swallowed up by their own self-consuming imperfection.

The fire's gleam shone far into the grove around, where damp, rotten leaves stuck up shining from the thin, slippery snow.

Then the people went into the tent and lay down on a large flat bed of reindeer hides and thin, soft birch twigs around the hearth.

The darkness covered the open fire's glow that was still blowing up one or other death flicker. The last red specks moved clumsily and drowned in the darkness.

But the cold brook went barking like a blind pup through the darkness, lived in endless unrest down in its bed, that crept crookedly and shadily down along the valley wall.

The reindeer that had already gotten a fairly thick winter pelt lay and rested on the soft moss. The herders lay under a bush, with their heads and hands pulled into their coat chests and with warm, longhaired dogs as blankets over their stomach and legs.

Lieđit (Boreal plants)

VII

Dense darkness supplies blood to the day's pale thoughts. In dense darkness the night owl's eyes sparkle, and lust swells in the predator's limbs. The juices trickle up from the sated pores and flow like tickling beads across every nerve …

Mother Biettar had lain awake the entire night, bitter from the most disgusting irritation that now Lasse was going to demand the six cows. How things had boiled in her, as soon as she noticed her son's fragile uncertainty towards Lasse! She became sick with rage and now lay and cursed and thundered beneath her reindeer pelt.

But then she broke into laughter and had to bite her coat sleeve so as not to awaken the others … There were still two stray and as yet unmarked calves in the herd! Wouldn't Lasse be satisfied with them and an honorably offered cow in addition; then he could travel back to the seminar again! … The devil was scraping in Mother Biettar's intestines, if he wouldn't be taken by the nose, the feeble badger, the cow blackmailer! … And that feature would at the same time tie a knot around him, so that for life and eternity he would become her inalienable slave. She would torment him, she would! … Then Elle could pester Biettar Oula with so many silly woman virtues as she wanted, – although to date she had still not spoiled the boy for Mother Biettar.

*   *

*

The postal people had taken off.

Lasse was still lying and enjoying himself under the reindeer skin hide. It was his first day. He took a prayer book that he had with him from "The seminar," and began to read in it.

"Is there anything in the prayer book about breaking promises and agreements?" asked Mother Biettar.

Lasse looked at her alarmed and with a dumb face worthy of pity.

"Yeah, you can just as well gape, you wretched owlskin!" hissed Mother Biettar and banged the coffee mill in the coals so the sparks flew up through the smoke hole. "No – damned, if you had earned three lemmings and far less three cows!" – She tentatively neglected to mention six.

Aslak could hardly keep from laughing. He had begun to think that Mother Biettar would take the bull by the horns; but Lasse together with this "taking the bull by the horns" seemed so funny to him.

"I shall have what I was promised," mumbled Lasse in a tearful voice.

"Been promised! – Yes, you are the one to speak about promises! – Oh, no! You aren't talking about promises with some scatterbrained tramp or other. … What is it you were promised, then?"

"That you yourself know well."

"But do you know what I promise you? – I'll hang you by your legs up in the pine tree here and thrash you on your rear, I will, if you make the least sign of trying to bring up demands, you miserable liar! … If I had known that you were such a lout as you turned out to be when you were before the court, then I would never have gotten mixed up in agreements with you! … But I consider myself too good to treat you according to your merits. Stand up now and follow me to the herd; I would rather settle up with you! – But eat first! – There you have a marrowbone, there is a hot sausage, and there you have fresh cooked back of a young reindeer. Eat marrow and blood and meat, boy!"

Lasse got up mechanically, ate and became bolder and more good-natured.

Then they went.

Both Elle and Biettar Oula had remained silent. Elle really wanted to warn Mother Biettar that she shouldn't delude Lasse into something crazy, but didn't dare – didn't take the trouble, for it was no use.

Mother Biettar had early this morning consulted with her son about her plan, and Biettar Oula had at the time thought that it was fine. But when Lasse opened his cold, poor eyes Biettar Oula was attacked by a delicate uncertainty, and then he would have preferred to see that Lasse got the six cows he had been promised; – then the tale would have been open-and-shut – in a way. But Mother was like a two-edged sword, and he had had to give in. His mind and will had become paralyzed last night – without his actually having felt it himself. He only felt that there was something wrong with him.

— Lasse who was still weak from his studying got sweaty and exhausted trying to keep up with the old witch; she hurried easily and without a sound like an owl: you could never hear her walking.

Arriving at the herd Mother Biettar held the following speech for Lasse: "There are three calves which are still unmarked. Two of them are cow prospects. Now you have two things to choose between. Do you want to accept the three calves and in addition an adult cow– or do you want to have nothing?"

Lasse who suddenly found himself face to face with his greatest fear – making a decision, and a rapid one at that – was sweating even more.

But so it was that the fear of missing out on the entire profit or being subjected to pursuing his rights through tribulations, conjured up an energy in him, and he answered yes.

But at the same time a tough, little dwarf seed of bitterness formed in him.

Suoidnestávrá (hay storage)

VIII

One evening Nikko Nille comes walking down the village's main road, proud and agitated. He walks a little bent forward and with his right shoulder up as if he were going to cross against a strong wind. This is because both his hands are occupied; with one he is leading a reindeer bull – there was no snow yet down here – and with the other one, his right hand, he is holding onto a corner of Æira Marit's kerchief. And Æira Marit sometimes pulls almost as much as the reindeer bull. Young girls are now so bashful themselves, anyhow need to show others that they are. But this time it isn't humbug from Æira Marit. She is trying to smile, but cannot. She just blushes and becomes completely unsteady in her walking by having to think about so much and feel so much: her little, lazy brain is not used to tall thoughts, and her heart would rather beat at a regular trot. Her otherwise so ready laughter muscles are as if paralyzed. For she must be thinking that she will soon have to leave father and mother and become Nikko Nille's wife … Sit in her own tent and sew coats and pants and all that is needed.

And now they're just a hundred steps from Jongo's house … Oh, God! People will look at her like someone who is a girlfriend and is getting married. It is so dizzyingly solemn … It is even good that it is as dark as it is.

They are just about to start down a little incline in front of Jongo's house, when Nikko Nille suddenly comes to a halt and pulls his sweetheart into himself. He is trembling like an aspen leaf; for he thinks that he clearly saw the old one's figure walk through a shaft of light outside the window and further toward the cow barn.

"What is it?" asks Æira Marit, and as bowlegged as she is, she can hardly keep her balance on her inward pointing feet.

"Didn't you see her?"

They stop a moment in breathless silence.

"There she goes!" whispered Nikko Nille.

"Oh – oh God!" Æira Marit groans and turns white as a corpse.

They keep their eyes on a path that leads to the churchyard; probably the apparition is on the way to the grave again …

No – she doesn't appear there …

Yeah, yeah! They have to walk on in the Lord's Name! – If only they can still get in as quickly as possible.

But suddenly they hear the midget's grunting voice shout from the wood hill: "Nah, where the devil did she go? – No sooner had we gotten the old sorehead down in the coffin than she leaps up again!"

The midget's burst of anger was accompanied by an exploding chorus of laughter whose contour Nikko Nille and Æira Marit could barely glimpse in the darkness, and that was following after the midget who was struggling to drag a large, coffin-like box over to the steps.

"Now it is the third time we are burying her," continued the midget. "But when we get her down into the chest then we'll nail the cover with sixteen nails and read the Lord's prayer seven times forward and seven times backward. And you, Erke, who are a brave cat, you shall go to the cemetery at midnight and find three whole owl turds beneath the large birch tree that the owl usually sits up in, and throw them one by one over the grave and say each time: "Sleep, old Zare! hu hu hu!"

And the midget darted around ardently and looked for the old one who was so obstinately against death. He had today well and fully sponged off the reindeer thieves in the northeastern district, and therefore he was so bold. After such a meal he usually always came to the southwestern part of the village and was then full of anger at the thieves' slaughter fests during the autumn nights, presumably because of pangs of conscience at having eaten such meat. But in the evening he didn't have time to preach penitence.

"Damn fellow!" the old one could be heard shouting hoarsely and ill-tempered outside the barn. Her prolonged movements had antagonized an ornery billy goat near her.

The midget ran to her and saved her with manly courage from the billy goat's attacks.

"That billy goat is going to be tied fast to the grave and stand watch there for eight days," he shouted. "Now – don't you want to get down in the coffin again, then? – Or do you first want to say farewell to Nikko Nille?"

But the old one laid it on the midget with her scolding. She, who with great care had been kept in the dark with regard to the rumors of her own death, flapped joyfully into Nikko Nille's arms, and with her mouth smiling at its friendliest width she said: "Is it you, my boy? … Hello, Hello!"

Although the connection had more or less dawned on Nikko Nille, still he had not yet gotten over his fright at the sight of the most real apparition he had ever seen in his life; – but he couldn't do anything other than take her by the hand. It felt like a corpse, and he was in a cold sweat. Æira Marit on the contrary didn't want to take the old one's hand at all; she just trembled and whimpered and was totally confused. An honest young man took her around the neck and assured her that the old one had never been dead, but up to the present always had been very much alive. At long last her whimpering began to abate. Suddenly her hand hit her mouth like a mechanical bulls-eye, and giggles sprouted out of her nostrils.

*   *

*

A couple of weeks later a hunter who for several days had stayed in an empty cabin, came down to the village and told the following:

One evening while he lay on the bunk bed and was falling asleep, or possibly he was already asleep, he heard a baby crying outside. It was pitch-dark in the cabin. He listens and looks toward the door. A little dot begins to grow light; it gets larger and larger, and finally takes on the shape of a little child … He understands then that it is an *Eahparaš*, a child born in concealment, and who is looking for its mother and wants to have a Christian baptism and Christian name.

He folds his hands and says: Your name shall be Nilas. Nilas! I baptize you in the name of the Father, Son and Holy Ghost!" – and he threw three bowls of water on it.

And *Eahparaš* disappeared and went to blessed repose.

From this formed the rumor that Æira Marit had concealed a birth. She had probably not been alone in her reindeer coat recently, they said. But a wise and worthy woman could testify that the whole thing was a malicious fabrication. And she spoke the truth. Æira Marit was not like that. Nikko Nille either.

Olbmoborranrássi (Angelica)

IX

Jussa had arrived yesterday.

He had been gone for many years. He now called himself Juhani; but here at home it didn't occur to anyone to call him other than Jussa.

The last part of the trip – from Lake Enare on – had taken all of eight days.

For the conditions had gotten poor; the last ten miles he had even had to carry his skis on his shoulders.

You see, it was towards the middle of May. Today he had dared to take a trip out to the riverbank. He had an uneasy feeling that he was playing the role of stranger at home. If he could just get past the first days! …

It had been damned disgusting to be a curiosity in Helsinki, and now he was going to suffer by being made a fuss over here at home! It was damned nauseating to be something in between.

And student of theology Juhani Jongo didn't realize it until he had said a good domestic oath. He was so shaken that he didn't even regret his sin.

But his blood picked up incredible speed when he suddenly caught sight of a woman who was coming directly toward him. He had recognized her, before his eyes captured her whole figure.

It felt so strangely sad this wave of memory that now, taking him by surprise, poured in over his soul …

Everything came apart in him, and he was floating along ... His eyes caught a foothold in the tips of her toes that aimed at tolerably dry points between the puddles ...

"May I be allowed to greet you, Miss Norum? – You can hardly remember me; but I once had the honor to speak with you." – He said it in Finnish.

"Whether I remember you!" – She laughed quite cheerfully. – "Besides it is not at all nice of you to assume that I shouldn't remember you."

"And you have gone astray up here in the mountains?"

"No – there isn't a trace of moral lapse in it, that I am up here. I have wanted to come up here since I was little. And this spring the minister and his wife here wrote that I should come and visit them. They are so gracious; they are the world's nicest people! And I like it so much here. Here the air is so pleasant, so fresh and light! ... Can you believe that the minister and his wife have two delightful children, a boy and a girl. They are so sweet and enjoyable! ... Yes, I've become an entirely new person here. Don't you think?" – She laughed. "Have you ever heard such questions! ... As if you should know how I have been before!"

Her liveliness was surprising and had a reassuring effect on Jussa. And what had become of the glance's melancholy power? ...

There are encounters that are followed by secret celebration, and festive happiness conceals so much ...

"But why do you want to become a Finnish minister, Mr. Jongo?"

"Speaking frankly, I don't even know myself."

"I think you should have become a Norwegian minister ... But if you become a minister in the neighboring parish in Finland then I will come and listen to you."

"Yes – if you will promise me that! – Then I will preach just for you, exclusively for you!"

"And then you must preach in Finnish, not in Sámi! ... Isn't there a stone church there – in the neighboring parish?"

"Yes."

"In a tiny little valley that cuts right into the desolate plateau?"

"Quite right!"

"And there is almost not a living soul in the valley except the minister?"

"No – almost not."

She looked down. Then she lifted her glance – quite slowly and let it slide into Jussa's eyes. "It must be strange … But how do you think it will go for you there?"

"The time, the grief! – I haven't become a minister yet."

"But you have to become a minister there – nevertheless!"

… Her glance swelled as the twilight in the forest.

Most people become less when the luster of the first festive expression is absorbed by the simple colors of intimacy. But in Elna's eyes the colors of intimacy were precisely deeper than all the luster of festiveness …

Then Jussa asked: "Why do you think I ought to become a minister precisely there?"

"Well – – –. I will tell you – –, I was down south a couple of years. People there were so cheerful and different than here. And now when I remember them from that time I saw them in Lafjorden, then I think that you ought to be a minister precisely there in the quiet valley that cuts right into the desolate plateau … And so I have always thought that Biettar Oula must be one of your listeners …"

"Always – you say?"

"Yes," she said and blushed suddenly. – "But when will you come and visit the minister? The minister and his wife spoke about you today. They really wanted to say hello to you … But now I must certainly go. I have taken a walk up onto the riverbank and looked at the river. Did you see how it is swollen!"

She said farewell and went.

Jussa stood and looked at her. Her young body seemed to play in overflowing joy of life.

Jussa stood with his senses suddenly on fire in the middle of spring's promising disquiet. – – "People there – down south – were more cheerful and different than here" … Yet one more time she came into view – on the churchyard hill; her hair shone golden and distant in the sunshine. So tall and so fair and so straight limbed! ... People there – in the white houses that become brighter southward along the coast and go in rows to the castles of the south, – and people here – in the dark forests and on the desolate plateaus! – People there headed toward the light and conquered the earth and the air, and the people here fled toward the darkness and oblivion ...

But Jussa was young and big and strong, and his nostrils were rinsed by a strong, liberating fragrance of earth. The air was full of heat haze and of the near and distant roar of running water.

It comes this spring like a hot fever dream one early morning hour. The sun undresses the earth in glaring brutality, throws a hot breath on every open spot and tickles the roots' juices to life under decomposing earth, yes, it fills all the sky's air with bacchanalian, festive smoke and everything living with hope and weak-willed rapture.

Jussa walked up over the riverbank, up to the birch underbrush.

A shaggy cow with wrinkly skin on its sprawling bones sniffed and munched greedily on the bloated buds and young branches. A dawning animal hope in its large, dull eyes. The animal stopped chewing, looked right out into the air and let its glance rest a long time on the haze ... And then it started to bellow with all its strength.

Long pools on the meadows streamed over the riverbank and sent yellow cascading jets down over the steep sandpit. Now and then a clump of shiny wet earth loosened and plunged splashing down toward the sand, drifted down into the open channel along the shore and pushed muddy stream eddies out toward the blue green edge of the ice.

White rapids sparkled in the forests on the valley sides; for from the day's first to the day's last hour the snow of the plateaus bathed in the heat of the sun and melted in streaming absence of resistance.

The woodcutters stood and hewed on the forest hills and the metal sound sang in the sun-trembling, spring friendly air.

Morša (walrus)

X

It is night – with light over the entire land, with sun reflections over the plateaus. And it is completely silent. Only Jussa's skis crackle against the crust.

Jussa goes over an outlying meadow on one of the headlands above the village. It is still snow-covered along the wooded slope on the south side.

The gun barrel has to be polished. He sticks the gun barrel in the snow and fires off a shot; a short, buried roar booms under the snow. The old stovepipe had almost taken off his collarbone. Sharp, quick wing beats could be heard in the bushes, and a couple hares go blinking through the edge of the forest. – He had nevertheless roused animals and birds up from their resting places.

He shoots a ptarmigan and gets hot from the shot's provocative roar, and the red blood on the snow-crust awakens an old blood thirst in him; as a boy he had learned from Biettar Oula to drink live animal blood. He puts the ptarmigan to his mouth, squeezes it and sucks the blood into himself. It's like the wine's first warmth streaming arousingly through the veins and gives his eyes a radiance. Every bush, all grassy hillsides and mountains and all animals and birds greet him with memories, and no, absolutely no controlling glance steals any of his freedom – God be praised! ... He shoots with gunpowder alone into the underbrush where he is sitting on a snowless hill in the middle of an outlying meadow and chewing resin. A morning greeting to all of you, a salute for all of us!

A hare swerves past. It meets a load of gun smoke and tumbles back with a leap into the air, but meets a new load and runs right toward him, stops and seats itself on its back legs. Jussa sticks a large, soft clump of resin into the rifle and shoots it right in the middle of the snout of the hare that rolls backwards, sniffs and shakes its snout and takes off. And Jussa bellows with laughter. "Excuse me!" – You could have done worse. You could have done worse.

— He has come to a small river that runs through a side valley.

Silently as a predator he twists through a willow shrub, up a hill. There could be ducks or gray geese in a pool at the river mouth.

But there weren't any.

The remnants of dense tracks in the thin, bluish slush on the ice on the big river tells him that Biettar Oula has recently gone north. No one else's herd could walk so wide and dense.

Jussa lies in the underbrush and thinks about many different things.

Lovesick male ptarmigans with voices crying in heat cackle around. He meows like an affectionate female ptarmigan. And the males come leaning forward, with embracing wings arching out and don't shrink from his large human body; for the heat chases them like a forest fire … large male animals, sniffing, chase in the tracks of the females and put their teeth in each other's throats in jealousy's blood wasting madness …

An ice floe turns toward the shore and sharp little pieces of ice trill against each other like ringing metal.

The sun already pours a thin breath of gold down along grassy hillsides and mountains. Elna! … "A stone church on the desolate plateau." You said it with heat haze in your eyes, with tinges of blood on your brow! … My hair is long and black, and my frock is like a black shadow that cuts my head from the pulpit; it cuts me from the people, from the world … Elna! If I could move time in, that time which is so far away, so that you followed along! … If you only tread on earth, Elna, then it sways more – – I can't stand it; my chest is burning, my eyes swim in fog … Elna! I can't stand it. The sun climbs slowly, and time melts my body, my soul! Good God, I can't stand it – – –

An animal's tramping crackles quickly on the snow crust. Jussa grips his rifle. A wolf comes trotting relaxed down from the side valley – with its snout in the reindeer tracks.

Jussa puts the rifle stock to his cheek, his eyes devour the colors of the hair, the corners of the mouth of the good-for-nothing fellow and the strong animal eyes' hard brilliance …

The shot bangs, and the wolf takes off with the speed of fear over the pool in the river.

He runs along, wades with cascades around himself over the river pool, crawls up onto the ice and chases on skis after the beast. He tenses all his muscles, sweat breaks out and the animal's large, red jaw urges him on into a bloodshot passion. The wolf is followed by blood stars in the snow while the one leg staggers. It throws its head back and aims white, strong teeth at him.

I don't give a damn about your teeth! I know you and your family!

They chase a side length of a river headland up over the ice, while the skis saw sharply into the snow crust, and gray smoke from hot breath whirls out of the wolf's rapidly pumping lungs.

The wolf hits land on the north side. Jussa splashes a few steps with his skis up over the bloody clay below the riverbank. – Lets his skis lie there and runs after the animal up the wooded hillsides. Often he loses sight of it, and his lungs fill his chest cavity all too strongly. But the wolf too must slow down: the wound hurts, and the blood loss is strong.

They cross over a steep scree slope on the mountainside, until the wolf has to stop in a mountain cleft. He loads the rifle with a good portion of powder and a homemade lead ball. Then he goes quite close to the wolf that is snarling from his jaw and struggling with its eyes. "Now I'm going to shoot you!"

The wolf gapes with its lower jaw and can't get it up again: it is crushed by the ball. He walks over and crouches down over the shaggy animal and drives his long dagger into its chest.

His hands tremble from exhaustion, and the sweat smarts in his eyes, while he flays the hide of the wolf and burns of animal predation.

Then he crawls up onto the crest of the mountain. Here he strips off all his clothing, wrings the water out and spreads them out to dry in the sun.

He sits with the wolf hide over himself and looks up the floor of the valley. Where the river winds in fast rapids around the chalet headland's great sand and gravel banks it is already ice free. He knows every cabin; he has been in all of them. He remembers the meadows that are usually richest in crowberrys and blueberries, – and the hillsides that later in the fall are usually heavy with blood red lingonberries. All paths that go over and around the hillsides he remembers. In the quiet, deep hollow above the backwater he has many a morning seen salmon shining silvery in the net. And all the ramshackle houses and tarns on the low plateau he knows. He has been everywhere here …

— Well – hasn't Biettar Oula gotten any further?

He sees smoke rise between a couple dilapidated shacks to the north. In a hurry he puts his clothes on and sets off.

Luopmánat (wild cloudberries)

XI

The dogs would surely have torn him to shreds if Biettar Oula hadn't come running and had threatened them with a ski pole and a flood of trilling oaths.

"Hm – isn't it Jussa?! And so huge you've become!"

"By God if it isn't Jussa!" Aslak shouted and came and greeted him quite moved. "Are you perhaps already fully trained?"

Jussa had to confess that there was still a long way to go.

"Yeah – then there won't be a thing left that you don't know!"

Oh, Jussa thought, there could always be a little left.

Biettar Oula explained that they had had to pitch temporary camp here since the cows had begun to calve earlier than expected. Now he and his people had already risked two days in a row. For there are cows who don't understand that a miracle has happened, but look at the little creature in the snow with hostile eyes and will trample it to death if you aren't careful right away to recharge the cow with mother's eyes by forcing it to smell the young one. The smell of the warm, little thing suddenly opens the lungs to a hot maternal spirit. The young one is licked and gets to suck cream-fat milk into itself. In the next hour it is ready to run with the mother and kick up a row in the snow.

— Biettar Oula went with Jussa to the tent.

Elle honored the guest with reindeer tongues and bone marrow and everything that was good.

And meanwhile Biettar Oula made inquiries about Finnish laws. He had now for several years functioned as a member of the township board, and he gave a clear account of the township's "budget." And that with an irreproachable tone in the official language.

… "So we have – the township board – thought about persuading a couple of rich reindeer Sámi in the west to move here to our parish. We must have people who can bring the communal budget into balance." – He enjoyed and underscored this turn of speech with a pause. "For the old mountain Sámi families here have nearly died out or are impoverished."

He had in recent years restrained himself completely toward his neighbors' reindeer. But the feeling of being a respected citizen in name and benefit was still so fresh that he sometimes had to look closer to home to make sure that it wasn't just an illusion. He enjoyed the new innate qualities in himself with visible pride – like a young woman who for the first time walks around with a living being in herself.

And with his conversion it had happened thus:

When Nikko Nille during his unsuccessful engagement journey down to the village brought along the miracle rumor, that one of his reindeer that had gone astray was found alive and uninjured in Biettar Oula's herd, it aroused so great an astonishment that the inhabitants in the northeastern neighborhood absolutely would not believe it. But Nikko Nille eagerly and incessantly assured that Biettar Oula himself was the first one who reported it to him that the reindeer was there. And that became little by little an irrefutable truth that Biettar Oula had now essentially become an honorable man.

When he then himself later in the winter came down to the village and stood face to face with his new reputation that shone with piety, he almost didn't recognize himself. He laughed up his sleeve – in the beginning. It was really promising to be regarded as an honorable man. And think, if he now also in reality had been that! – The vanity captivated him to the extent that he completely seriously decided to undergo an inner purification.

And then his progress began; his already earlier so polite language became more and more elegant, and Biettar Oula landed in the lower court. And such a fuss was made over him that there was no end to it.

The preachers fought over which of them had the credit for his conversion, while others claimed that the whole thing was Elle's work …

"But how is my old friend Nikko Nille?" Jussa asked.

"Hm," smiled Biettar Oula. "He had a tendency to be unhappy, you know. His old one died only a couple years ago, and by then he had wasted everything he owned and had. He stole reindeer like a wolf and went to prison. And now he busies himself with a little fishing down by the sea. That is of course all impoverished mountain Sámi's last way out. Yeah, yeah! It couldn't really have gone any differently. The man was haunted and obsessed by misfortune. We occasionally give him an animal to butcher. For it is a shame for a man who has seen better days."

"So then he didn't get married to Æira Marit after all?"

"No, – she married someone else and has a baby every year – in competition with the best cows."

Elle had to smile at that, where she sat with her third child in her ample lap and nursed it from her sumptuously rich bosoms. She smiled blushingly roguishly: the intimation flattered her sense of the feminine calling.

"And there we have Lasse," said Biettar Oula, in that Lasse came crouching down into the tent door and threw himself down on a reindeer skin. He had turned into an excellent fellow. What a guy, who has taken good care of his reindeer! He has over the years become a prosperous man."

Jussa felt unpleasantly touched that Biettar Oula himself condescended to flatter Lasse. But Lasse sat and enjoyed the flattery with the most demanding face.

There was an excruciatingly fragile disquiet at Biettar Oula's many attentions toward him, an unconcealable need to see Lasse put on a nice face.

Jussa's old compassion toward Lasse was transformed into a strong antipathy; for behind his miserable, arousing pity he glimpsed now an anemic gray-black maliciousness that all of Biettar Oula's disarming charm could not overcome. It was an excruciating sight to see Biettar Oula, strong as an animal, beset with this half-finished outcast of a person, whose early aging skin and flesh lacking strength seemed to be of a more than commonly coarse material.

— Jussa got ready to leave. But Biettar Oula and little Andi who now had grown to become so much like his father, led him first into the herd and captured a large bull.

"This is for you as thanks for the visit," said Biettar Oula. "And if you become a minister in the neighboring parish, then I'll come and listen to you preach God's word."

Rievssahat (ptarmigans)

XII

On the way home Jussa saw the ravens flapping and circling around the wolf carcass up on the scree slope; they shrieked hoarse and incessantly, but didn't dare to
sink all the way down; for presumably a fox had taken it into possession.

— The river had risen severely, and the ice had gone up in several places. He
couldn't get over here, but had to go over the headlands on the north side.

Later in the evening when he stopped on a hill above the village headland, the
ice was already in full swing.

He saw people standing out on the spit of land – in front of them Elna in a
light coat. Her hair shone golden in the evening sun. He waved with the wolf skin.
They waved again. Elna went right up to the edge of the riverbank and waved; the
minister's wife had to hold her by the coat, so that she wouldn't fall off.

The ice floes boomed and ground against each other and thrust up white walls
of ice powder. The crowding increased, and the speed became less and less. The
enormous, dammed up masses of water had buried the edges of the sand near the
river, and of the outlying meadow on the headland on this side only a few willow
bushes could be seen. But far back in the bay where the headland began, in the
meadow, there were quiet open waters where one or other ice floe sailed that now
and then got stuck in the trees inside. Of the village headland's otherwise high,
steep riverbank there was only a relatively small terrace left above the water.

A long, giant ice floe cut slowly but irresistibly self-important through the mass piles and thundered and ground its front end against the hill Jussa was standing on, while white masses of metal-sounding ice needles piled up on the shore. The upper end began to swing toward the village headland – and there lay the giant – like a huge bridge over the river. The water opened up a couple places below and boiled in black current eddies.

Jussa put on his skis and let the reindeer pull him over the ice bridge; the animal hauled away so that the loose slush sprayed noisily on the tips.

"But good grief then, Jongo, how you frightened us!" said Elna. "How can you hit on something so evidently perilous as to go over the floating bridge of spray there?"

"To show off – of course!" – And then he whispered in Finnish and in such a roguish tone: "And frankly speaking: if you hadn't been standing here, then –."

"Yes, but you must never again risk your life for my sake. That is – –."

"No, no, young lady! It will not happen again."

He heard himself how his voice suddenly became hard; a sudden shiver tensed his nerves and wouldn't let go.

"That is – – –;" but in his penitent bewilderment he couldn't come up with an explanatory and apologetic word.

"It is surely not your intention to say something such as that it would be another matter if I got special permission from you to risk my life for your sake?"

This raw remark finished it completely with her, precisely because she herself so sincerely regretted that she had expressed herself awkwardly.

He said farewell, pulled the reindeer close with strength that had increased from the abrupt turn in his soul, – and left.

Dorski (cod)

XIII

Elna and Jussa sat on the headland above the village. They sat in the shadow of a group of willow bushes that stood on the outer edge of an outlying meadow. The broad, low sand edge by the river was light in the sun's gleam; small discs of mica glittered as if they were actually silver.

Plump bumblebees swayed lazily around the willow bushes' yellow catkins and over the bluebells in the grass. The summer's afternoon sun shook a hint of light into the trees' shadows.

Jussa felt an inner need to thank God for the summer and for her who lay with her face against his chest, and whose soul's ardent devotion had consecrated the summer.

— But into this beautiful silence snuck a gentle sob up from her chest. The first shot of happiness is fragile and sensitive to cold like a flower. It is hurt in the cold and bad weather and dies in the sunshine …

Jussa didn't really know why she was crying; but was drawn along by her trembling, and his voice was moist with tears, when he asked her: "Why are you so grieved, Elna?"

"You mustn't be angry, dear Juhani! … I must tell you something." – Her silent weeping became a painful sobbing. "I think that you now and then are so distant from me, and then I always get so afraid!" – and she pressed into him as if she were afraid there might be a distance between them.

Jussa could answer nothing at first. Something had come over him suddenly. Their conversations until now had been carefree and unreflected like the sunlit nights' awakened dreams.

"Are you dissatisfied, Elna?"

"Yes – I don't really know … Dear Juhani, don't be mad at me!" – She took him around the neck and looked into his eyes: "How black your eyes are, Juhani! … Promise me that you will never inflict anything bad on me! – Do you remember the first time I spoke with you? – You remember that I said that I had such a desire to travel up here, – although I was almost afraid, I was afraid of the land here – and people like Biettar Oula … Later I didn't think so much about it, – not until I met you this spring … Juhani! – Forgive me that I say it – it wasn't just joy for me to see you again. Also the anxiety awakened in me this strange dread from my childhood days. But I only realized it that time you drove over the ice and got angry with me, because I happened to say something I didn't mean. You got such a terribly hard radiance in your eyes. – It wasn't just the regret that I had offended you that drove me to search for you – I hurt so much then! – It wasn't just the regret – It was – – not because I want to compare you with a snake; but I have heard or read about small birds that fly right into a snake's jaws, – although fear holds them back. But perhaps it is just the fear that chases them into the dreadful. I was and am not afraid of you, not like that. But the anxiety, the anxiety! Juhani. It gave me no peace, never a moment's peace! But you were mean that time, you avoided me, – I perhaps made myself laughable in people's eyes; but I didn't care about it. The minister's wife tried to talk sense into me. Sense! What did I care about sense! Once in a while I caught a glimpse of you, and then I always thought that you had something around you, something that I cannot really explain. Yes, there was something of loneliness in here; it almost made me seasick.

And she pressed herself again trembling into him. "And yet – yet I love you so infinitely much, Juhani! I love you helplessly much. Perhaps that is where my anxiety comes from, – and because you are sometimes so infinitely far away from me! … If only you didn't have this awful wasteland around you!"

She was silent. But Jussa wouldn't say anything.

One awakens to a strangely far-reaching consideration when ones course of life suddenly swerves into a layer of frost.

Jussa thought about her who had her lineage in a family of people that was the world's most beautiful and streamed in the majestic might of masses over the earth and were its bright gods. And he thought about the solitary cabins and smoky houses in the dark, desolate forests along the polar sea and about the people who lived in them. He himself was born one dark evening, while his mother was gathering reindeer moss above the wooded slope. They had had to spend the night there, and the dense darkness was the first thing his eyes absorbed … Had the sea poured its crushing weight into Elna's eyes?

— "Juhani! – Do you love me? Oh, you must love me! … Do you remember when I finally once met you here in the forest? I wished I was far away, and you certainly did too. But we couldn't get past one another. You were so big and strong and dark when you suddenly popped up from the underbrush! Do you remember how I shook when you took me by the hand? I got tears in my eyes; I didn't cry; but – it had such a terribly intense effect on me."

"I saw you that night, Elna. The night before I met you. The early morning you were bathing in the dewy grass in the minister's garden. You had a light blue coat over your shoulder."

"Did you really see me? – That wasn't nice of you, Juhani." Her face and neck flushed a little, and she smiled with a mix of embarrassment and pleasure.

"You were beautiful, Elna, when you stood there a while and looked right into the sun. You had a luster in your hair – and on your light blue coat."

"Was I beautiful? – Love me, Juhani! You must love me!"

Her sleeves had slipped up. Jussa felt the arteries' beat in her white arm that was wrapped around his neck, and he saw the fair woman's young, rich body breathe under her light summer clothing.

"The sun and the air were so warm that night; I wasn't able to sleep. I thought about you and became even warmer from that. I had to bathe in the dewy grass; it was so nice and cool."

Then they were silent again.

"Do you maybe hate me, Juhani?"

Nor to this did Jussa reply. However, he asked: "How do you regard the relationship between us? Tell me, Elna!"

"Relationship? … Relationship! … That is true – we have never spoken about it! Can you understand that? Why haven't we ever spoken about it?"

"Presumably because there has never been any relationship between us. And presumably never can be either."

Elna hardly noticed it herself that there was a sigh of release that shot up from her chest. "But I want to have your love of me when I travel away – all your love, Juhani!"

But when she bowed down to catch his glance, she suddenly pulled back: he had gotten a steel look in his eyes.

"Juhani!" …

"Are you going to travel down the river, Elna?"

"Yes! – Haven't I told you that before?"

"No – you haven't … You didn't tell me that before. And would probably not have done so now if I hadn't asked you about it."

They were silent. Elna tore nervously at the grass.

Then she said: "The bailiff will be on a vacation trip to the south."

"Oh."

There followed a suffocating pause.

Then Jussa said: "He lives at the river mouth. I have seen him only a single time. Once many years ago when he almost convicted Biettar Oula, – he whom you once said cast a spell over a woods if he only walked through it."

"I'm not going down the river to meet him. "You mustn't be mad at me, Juhani! You must not be mad at a poor girl like me!"

"If you are afraid of me then you ought to go. And then a sincere thanks to you for a pleasant time, Elna!" – He squeezed her hand warmly. "One best avoids evil by shrinking from it."

She sank into his grasp during hectic sobbing. "No – that cannot be true, that we are now going to part forever, – not forever, Juhani! … Oh, help me, my God!

I cannot live without you, Juhani! I cannot. My soul will die in me, and I will fade away alive and young. – Don't look like that at me! Be nice to me, Juhani!"

She sank down with eyes closed. "Let me kiss you one more time! ... Feel, how my heart pounds! ... I think I am sick. Don't do anything mean to me! ... Oh no, it is perhaps futile to demand that promise from you. – Wipe my brow too! ... Thanks! ... It's stuck at the neck; I'll loosen it myself ... Your breath warms my chest so wonderfully! ... Thanks, Juhani, thanks for your being good to me!"

*   *

*

Jussa was sitting alone again. And he sat there a long time.

A hateful thought and a hard word cut into a loving person like a bite from an insane animal. Ones vitality is sapped by an unquenchable thirst for a reconciliation; but as soon as it is suspected to be near one moves back shyly ...

— Jussa awakens by hearing the polers' blows against the gunwale. He looks up.

Down there – around the promontory point on the other side come a man and a woman poling up the broad, evenly running river. They have just gotten to where the protruding sandbank below the promontory point narrows and goes over to a sandpit that lifts weakly and gets steeper going up.

The man who is in a white shirt and has a woven, red belt around his waist, stands at the back end of narrow, flat-bottomed and high-prowed boat, whose new wood below a thin, bright layer of tar shines red in the sun. The woman stands at the fore end. Her very short jacket of striped, quilted material is wet in front right up to the chest. They pole in step, they move each time the mandatory three strokes up the long, white, smooth poles and put stress on them with practiced weight of force so the rapids snarl around the bow, and the waves roll noisily over the stony gravel on the shore.

The sandpit casts echoes from their voices, from the poles' regular beats against the gunwale and from the shiny tin pail's clatter. They are going up to the summer cabin.

The swallows have bored holes for their nests in the sandpit, right up under the leaning edge of the heather, which is held up by in-woven birch and juniper roots. They shriek out and in and gorge in a mob of mosquitos and blackflies.

The reflections from the riverbank, the wooded slopes and the mountain ridge stick out from the dying waves from the boat and taste the shining blue-white sea.

*   *

*

The next day Jussa walks down the village that is resting in summer solitude. Children and old folks are at the summer chalet. The timber floaters and cod fishermen have gone up the river.

The women sit barelegged in front of open windows and doors spinning wool and weaving homespun. The aired out and scoured walls cast an echo of the voices and of the looms quick raps. Sometimes a gust of wind comes, and the grass on the meadows flows sparkling in the sunshine.

… Should he perhaps turn back anyway and say farewell to her?

— Oh no …

He is lying in the deciduous woods on the headland below the village; he is no further from the riverbank than that he can see the river if he raises himself up … Then he hears the echo of strokes. – What if he walked down onto the shore and said farewell to her?

"Row to the shore," he hears her say to her boatmen. Jussa runs further into the woods and hides there.

A little later Elna comes up on the riverbank, stares a while expectantly at the place where Jussa had lain … and runs down again.

Dálbmeluokta (Talvik)

XIV

Over the years Lasse became more and more difficult to satisfy. Not because he ever made threats: his indignation that he had been put off with three calves and a poor cow, never blew up into a great effort demanding a release in an outburst of anger. But powerless as this long suppressed bitterness of his was, then it made him anyway – and just for that reason – capable of preserving an anemic standoffishness vis-à-vis Biettar Oula. Mother Biettar had managed to hold her own against him as long as she was healthy. But when her health began to decline, he got more breathing room, and his oppressive sliminess received a fresh infusion from his memories of her ruthless obstinacy and it left its mark in his eyes, in his face, in all his actions of his feebly passive obedience.

And he, who never before in his life had been granted power over another human being, could not afford to yield in the least his hold over Biettar Oula. His shred of original human love died in this dog bite – in any case, toward Biettar Oula. Now he had the upper hand over the strongest person he knew; and he would squeeze! And gradually he himself learned to understand that it was precisely this bloodless gray-black in him that could only be suspected, but never came into view externally, – that there was force in. And his two cents in that direction he made the best use of.

This essence of his meant that Biettar Oula could not get around to reaching him in time. This was something that Biettar Oula hoped would disappear over time. He wasn't used to cajoling and petty, distrustful attentiveness. Envy and that sort from his side he was used to overlooking.

But in this case Biettar Oula had not been attentive to what had happened inside him while Lasse was away.

The beginnings of his present weakness vis-à-vis Lasse he got during the interrogation. It was a real battle to stand so near the possibility of having to perjure himself. Then, practically speaking, he became acquainted for the first time with fear. And already the first night the small twinges of bad hunches began that Lasse would become a nasty fellow for him. Later he blew them off. Silly delusions! But – then he could anyway sometimes catch himself standing breathless and thinking about this business with Lasse.

Lasse came, and the twinges increased – Biettar Oula almost unaware.

This inner undermining went on for years.

But when his reputation changed so suddenly – unbeknownst to him too –, and he climbed from rank to rank and ended up on the township board, then he became vigilant, alert, sensitive, even suspicious. And then it dawned on him how terribly much Lasse's evil eyes and cold and oppressive being had taxed his resistance. He had lost all self-control and understanding of the effect of the expedients: he showered Lasse with gifts and laughable attentions – and that, although he had more than adequate experience that even a guardian angel made no impression on Lasse's impenetrably thick crust of icy numbness, yes, just added new layers to it.

He became bewildered and helpless in his fumbling for a way out to get the upper hand with Lasse.

Then one night something happened to Biettar Oula.

He had lain awake for a long time: he had begun to be afflicted by sleeplessness recently. Now he lay quite stiff, with all his muscles tensed. Then he slowly began to tremble – like a gentle sigh from a wall clock about to strike, and suddenly he twitched violently, a gleam of light brushed past his eyes – was it lightning? He sat up, put his hand on his heart to convince himself that he was still alive, – stared around himself ... Yes, he was in the tent, – and Elle swelled up and with calm breaths under the pelt beside him ...

The next night he lay in the same way and awaited with anxiety a repetition of what happened the previous night. But he tried to lie with his eyes open: maybe sleep would steal a march on him … Then he sees a gray spot; is he lying with his eyes open? – Yes … But the gray spot in the dark a ways in front of his eyes he sees anyways … Suddenly it moves closer and is transformed at the same instant into Lasse's face – with bloodshot eyes and more pallid and anemically gray-black than any other time … One moment, then it is transformed into Biettar Oula's own face, also pallid and gray-black …

He sat up and groaned. Elle awakened: "What is it, Ovllážan?"

He crept in under her pelt and hid his face in her arms, fearful and trembling like a little child …

— And at this time an old experience came up in his memory. A great many years had passed without him having given it a thought. But now it came, not just as a memory, but with all its own crushing strength … He again got the desire to rip the nostrils off Elle, pinch her in the thigh and himself picture how it would crackle in the bailiff's bones, if he … But then he became frightened: he couldn't bring it off, leave the battlefield as the victor. The courage always betrayed him in his mind – always – and the consequences came to haunt him … oh no! He hoped to avoid such … Although! – – The bailiff had taken the gray wolf's daughter from Jussa. Everyone had said that she was going to become his wife … So who knows!

– – – –

Fálesbivdu (whale hunting)

XV

One autumn they lay with the herd by a mountain lake just south of the inland valley, about sixty miles southeast of the village.

— One evening the herders' yoiking fell silent.

Old Mother Biettar was near death.

The herd's rumbling past the tent without the usual shouts from the herders sounded so depressing – like a soughing of spirits – and concentrated gravity of the hour:

"Can't you yoik a little, then! – Girje! hush!"– She fenced with her stick and clawed in the thick-haired reindeer hides she was tucked down in.

Andi – Little Andi as he was still called – sat on the other side of the hearth. Every time the smoke from the steaming, raw birch branches rose together, he looked past the kettle. But his grandmother's eyes shone so bright and stiff against the black tent wall. Now he wanted to try to refrain from looking several times. And he sat there and moped wretchedly and depressed, he didn't even have tears.

Elle sat with the New Testament and Psalm book in her hand.

The tongues of northern lights quivered in great loops under the vault of heaven.

"Now the sky is burning! – Let us flee!" – And Mother Biettar's eyes stared up through the smoke hole ... "Stamp the blood down in the snow, Oula! ... Even out all the tracks! Can you change the mark? – No? – Cut the ears off then!"

Biettar Oula turned pale. These words had been his mother's refrain every time they had slaughtered an unfamiliar reindeer in the old days.

"Read in the testament, Elle!"

Elle paged with numb fingers in the soiled book. But the smoke was unpleasant and the firelight poor, and she hadn't concerned herself with the reading since she went before the minister.

"Couldn't you say a little prayer, then?"

Yes – if only she could think of something!

"Shouldn't we sing a hymn, Elle?"

"God Alone in Heaven." They both knew it so well. But only one verse.

"I think we should sing it again," said Biettar Oula. They sang it four times and became warm at heart.

If they could now say a few of God's words too!

Elle began to say the Lord's Prayer. She didn't really get all of it; but she was able to say most of it ...

"Jesus," came slowly from the old ones lips.

And just as Biettar Oula opened the tent door to fetch in a little wood, old Mother Biettar drew her last breath, as the cold autumn gust from the plateau rushed over her bed.

"Didn't she say Jesus?"

"Yes!"

— — —

— There were no skiing conditions yet, and it was impossible to move the body down to the village.

A couple days later her earthly remains were laid down in a sled and buried in a rock-strewn slope higher up.

Her old hired man Aslak read the burial ritual from the Psalm book. Then he built a large stone barrow over the corpse so that predators couldn't come and eat it up.

Várggát (Vardøhus)

XVI

There had been slush for a while. And when the cold commenced, the slush froze to ice on the reindeer moss. The animals had trouble finding bare spots and roamed far and wide over the heights around the tarn.

One of the days after Mother Biettar's death Biettar Oula and Lasse stood outside the tent. Lasse was going out to herd, but stood as usual and stalled for a long time.

Then Biettar Oula says: "Do you see the reindeer there on the heights on the other side of the lake? – It would perhaps be best to chase them to the south end of the lake. It's better grazing there."

Yeah … Yeah – – Lasse would do it …"The ice is probably strong enough now that I can walk over."

Biettar Oula gritted his teeth. The thoughts that had been on his mind in recent days suddenly were on the verge of becoming reality, yes, before he had had time to become used to them.

"Yes, it is, quite certainly." His voice deserted him; he had to swallow the words.

Lasse began to walk over the ice. The tracks in the new fallen snow became longer and longer. Biettar Oula stood and watched. Short booms were heard in the ice, occasionally longer crashes … Biettar Oula shook.

Lasse was already approaching the steep rocky face on the other side ... Then Biettar Oula runs down to the shore and gasps for air to shout to Lasse that he must turn back, – – – but the sound won't come up from his throat, – he crouches and gets out a yell just at the moment when the ice breaks ... A cap was floating in the open channel; it moved slowly from the bubbles that rose up ... And then everything became still. There was deep water below the steep, rocky face.

Skuolfi (owl)

XVII

The eagle-owl is among the quiet creatures in this desolate land. It is grand in its loneliness, and it is an ominous event when it approaches the abodes of humans. For it comes to remind one about "that sin, you know."

Biettar Oula who had now begun to shun people and never appeared in the tent until far into night, sat one evening at dusk on the steep slope of a high scree that dropped precipitously down to the river. The valley bottom was already full of darkness; but the light over the plateau merged more and more into a golden, green shining gleam over the mountain line to the west, and the distances moved into each other everywhere.

Biettar Oula has gathered a large pile of dry, tarry pine roots on the steep slope of the scree. That terrible thing could come, and the fire is a good defense when the darkness has swallowed the plateau …

A hollow hooting is heard "Huhuhu." Biettar looks up and catches sight of a pair of sparkling pupils uppermost on top of a weather beaten pine tree that rises up from the scree …

It's the eagle-owl. And the contours appear as large as an eagle against the night-gray sky. It's sitting so immovably still, wrapped in a huge feather cloak. The mottled breast shines gray like the transparent skin on a corpse, and the glowing pupils in the humanlike face stare impassively at the large shape on the scree's steep slope. The eagle-owl turns its head a little; the angular rays of the pupils jump a bit, – and everything dies again in an impassivity that takes the breath away …

Biettar Oula's chest is filled with a shuddering desire to burst this desolate silence of death with a large animal's thundering roar. ... But the roar won't come up from his chest, and he has to be silent ...

Finally, the eagle-owl lifts its wings and sails ghostly and soundlessly down into the mist-filled, dense darkness of the valley ...

It is the message of death. The third time it will come accompanied by its and the eternal darkness' master ...

A whistling is heard from the plateau. It is the autumn storm.

— Biettar Oula gropes his way to the pine root pile. He tears off a fire stick against his trousers, a prick of phosphorous light feeds in the darkness and quavers and whistles between his shaking hands ... He lights the pile ... The autumn storm comes and pours onto the bonfire's flames large, intense waves against the powerfully surging masses of smoke with tinges of crackling red. It sparkles and flashes in the melting embers, and dog howling from the other side of the valley pierces its misery through the darkness ... The reflection of the flames shoots far into the black air over the valley and laps the scree too that is hanging and fluttering shining wet in the depths of the darkness.

Biettar Oula jumps and dances, waving his arms around the bonfire. The blood rolls in sensual shudders through his arteries ... "Ice is strong," he whispers into the storm that howls over the forest in the valley and blows one or other flute tone into the thin, dry bushes on the scree ...

It wails in the swaying forest and groans in the darkness.

"I've killed him," he whispers into the storm, and the insanity burns in his eyes, while he jumps back and forth through the bending flames ... He stops and listens. "Now my words sail with the storm." – He puts one ear to the ground and listens. "If they only don't meet anyone! ... Hush! – Now they splash against a window!" ... "Who have you killed? – Who have you killed, Biettar Oula?" – But Biettar Oula's words sink no more. They just lie there on the floor, and when the bailiff lights a match he does not see more words than "I have killed him" ... But on the wall he discovers "Ice is strong." The words have crashed so hard that they have sprayed rays around themselves ...

Then Biettar Oula whispers into the storm: "If you betray me, then I'll knock the marrow out of your bones!" …

People who had tents on the other side of the valley and had been awakened by the dog howling stood and looked terror-stricken at the waving figure who flew around the spewing blazes.

Suddenly the bonfire topples out over the steep slope, and the live embers are smashed falling down along the scree and scatter in a long tongue down into the darkness. A crash of a rolling stone tears a thunder of loosening scree along, and the ice bursts, and the water is lifted and breaks the surface with a swelling of sighs that groan in a thousand rays up along and down along the ice, around in a ring and above, dies out one place, but comes to life far away, turns back and meets itself and shores up a large lamenting bang with rejuvenated force. The dead water that recently ran so passively and calmly under the ice, breaks in a choking fit and stretches breathlessly until it at long last is exhausted … Then it becomes silent. But one more time a barking shriek is heard far down, – and in the wake of the last tripping crash comes a sound from the steep slope, takes the dying tone of the soughing, climbs to a wild yoiking, sweeps along the dog howling and whirls ungodly words into the storm …

Ealibat, lottit etc. (Animals, birds, etc.)

XVIII

Late one winter evening Jussa sits by the window and looks out. The leaning wooden crosses around the large stone church barely stick up from the snow surface. The snow goes almost up to the church's narrow windows and lies thick and swelling over the roof.

The birch stalks up along the valley side; but it is as if it becomes snowed under on the way, and the snow gets to hug the entire, dozing low crest and conquer the whole plateau beneath itself.

The winter road that goes up through the little valley is also half snowed under. The few families who live further above the church do not have many errands to run out in the world. Almost all of Jussa's parish children, you see, live down by the great border river spread miles apart.

— Thus he has sat every evening since he took over the call last fall – listened for sound, had a very strong urge to shock the silence with his own voice, but has never gotten around to doing it …

Thus, when it returns, this great urge to cry out, he goes over and opens the dining room door to listen to the old Finnish servant girl sing spiritual songs in the kitchen. Like the old, faded office furniture she has been inherited from minister to minister all of whom true enough only played guest roles here.

In a little while he goes back and sits by the window …

Old Marja has gone to bed, and the full moon is just swelling up from the crest of the hill.

And Jussa is still sitting by the small-paned window.

The church's broad shadow suddenly sticks forth a little tongue that moves by fits and starts over the snow on the ground and disappears into the spire's long shadow.

Jussa intensifies his vision.

Over at the cemetery fence stands a man caring for a reindeer. He tethers it, fastens his skis and takes the path to the parsonage directly across the ground.

The tall, heavy figure comes right up to the window.

Jussa gets up.

The man stops and looks in. Under the frosty eyebrows shines a look that Jussa seems to recognize.

Jussa tries to open the fast frozen window; but the man winks deprecatingly. "Hush!" – He puts his face right into the window. "Are you alone, Jussa?" he whispers.

"Yes. Isn't it Biettar Oula? ... Walk over to the door and then I'll come and open up." – – –

Biettar Oula's sobbing had gradually changed to a mild, muffled weeping. The words writhed and struggled up from his throat; they sank down and again popped up, all while they pumped out his life's great and ready-to-burst sore subject. The big, strong man had not cried since he was a boy, and his crying was therefore so much more violent and painful ...

—"I was shouting to him that he should turn back; but it was as if something was holding my voice back, although it filled my chest, so that I was about to suffocate ... And it was surely an evil thought that gagged my voice ... It is the thought, my evil thought, that I killed him! – It'll never be otherwise no matter how much I try to turn it around! ... And then I couldn't take it any more. I couldn't, Jussa! I had to travel here. I dared not go to the minister at home. And you I have known from the time you were quite little."

They had put out the lamp, and the moon was shining on his pale, teary face where he sat on the floor, and leaned his head against Jussa's knee.

"It isn't because your sin – this evil thought you are speaking about – in itself is worse than most of our sins and thoughts, – that is not why you have suffered so much. But it is because your mind was insane that time, your entire soul was hurting and in pain, and every thought swelled up in your conscience like bad seeds in rich soil … Well, let sin be sin! – But rest assured that the dreadfulness of that sin that has ravaged in you, it has carried you up to God – like a huge, breaking wave that pours onto a drowning human and saves it … Don't you feel yourself that you are closer to God?"

Yes – Biettar Oula did so. If he thought more about it then he was certain about the way to God.

And they knelt down by the window and prayed to God.

"And do you believe that I can partake of the sacrament?"

"Just now you can."

Jussa put on his cassock, and the two of them walked to the church …

— Biettar Oula lay on his knees in front of the altar.

In the large, dark church burned to lonely altar candles. The flames were fanned by the cold draft that drifted up to the altar along the walls and froze the minister's and Biettar Oula's hot breath. The large, empty room under the high vault gave an echo of the minister's pure, muffled voice, while he intoned the founding words. The night's gravity, the lonely human's sin and the holy ritual gave his voice soul and bedewed its warmth.

And when the words sounded thus: "He also took the chalice," Biettar Oula's face lit up with a peaceful clarity …

– – –

Already before the dawn's early light Biettar Oula had left. He drove up the ice on the river.

Nissonat, mánát (women, children)

XIX

Jussa suddenly gained renown as a converted minister. He let his copious, black hair grow long, and each successive Sunday his face became thinner and more pale and seemed to shine from a furious, hidden joy over his lonesome existence in the silence of this desolate place. His calm, softhearted mildness toward people he met privately, surely made people feel good in his presence, but without familiarity's regular comfort: the introspective remoteness that shone out of his countenance and being, would never move closer …

— But one Sunday – it was later in spring – it seemed to people that he actually was swaying to and fro from disquiet, disquiet that could not be concealed. What had happened to him? His words were uninhibited, often hard, yes probably not always entirely Christian either: he spoke about things that people did not know anything about, and that aroused indignation. The minister ought not to boast about knowing a little more than the simple common man. Ministers who were of the right sort of people, never condescended to such …

Jussa had heard something about Elna.

There were rumors about something that had been raked up in the strong-rooted memories from his youth, turned his inner being inside out, so he staggered in ecstasy and spoke to walls: it turned inside out the most distant corners of his memories, shook everywhere, found peace nowhere, – because he himself didn't know where that something should be pinched off. There were way too many possibilities …

— Elna's husband had had to travel alone to the south. She had not been able to get ready – –

— There were myths about the bonfire and the noise that night. The mountain Sámi had heard words that also involved the bailiff, and they were bad words. They found their way to the bailiff too, and when he remembered Biettar Oula's remarkably large, dark figure he became uneasy. This and the fact that his physical and mental health had been injured by the many winters of clammy darkness and the many beakers of comfort, caused him to have to travel to the south, even before he had gotten a new post. But Elna still had not been able to get ready …

Then it was told.

– – –

The next Sunday Jussa stands in the pulpit and speaks about the deaf and dumb whom the Lord gave the ability to speak and hear.

Once his glance brushed a woman far back by the door, and he began to reach for words. Another time his eyes seek her, he is shaken by a fumbling sensation: she is in a Sámi costume, but – –

… He stops, presses his lips together, squeezes the ritual book between his hands and fastens his glance on his white knuckles …

Then he said the following:

"Someplace out by the great world ocean there is an underwater hole inside a steep mountain wall – how far in, no one knows.

At ebb tide you can see its dripping and green glittering vault disappear into black vapor, and the breakers die inwards in a distant swallow.

At flood tide the chasm's upper lip is under water; but every time the breakers recede, part of the chasm opens with a spewing roar – until new breakers are lifted, and the chasm slurps water and everything floating close by into itself with a gurgling noise.

This hole is said to have miraculous effect on the deaf and dumb.

A stranger from far away who in childhood years had been deaf and dumb, came one day to try the latest remedy, the wonder.

140

No one really knew, where he was from. But a fair, young woman said that he was from the boggy plateaus to the east …

The strange man rows out to the miraculous chasm.

The breakers shove the boat back and forth; and then the chasm makes a large pull so that a cold, tickling air stream is thrust up from the deaf and dumb person's lungs, his tongue loosens, he expels a shriek, a jubilant shriek before the voracious abyss; his ears are opened, and he listens in dizzying joy to the sound of the sea and turns the boat away from the chasm's decisive gulp …

He rows back.

And as he walks up from the beach and is overwhelmed by the opened senses' play, he meets the fair, young woman. "I can speak! The Lord be praised! I can speak, and I can hear!" and he is going to embrace her; for he feels so thankful toward all. But she pushes him away: "Get thee hence, human! – What do I care whether you can speak and hear or not!"

He wanted to have said: "No, no! – You are right. I ask your forgiveness; I didn't mean it maliciously." – But at the same instant his tongue again became paralyzed: he wasn't able to say it. Nor did his ears hear any more.

But the only words they had heard since the last time his mother's voice sounded in his childhood soul, that deafness continued to separate from life's great song, – the only words were: "Get thee hence, human! What do I care whether you can speak and hear or not?"

The stranger from far away rowed again out to the underwater hole, but this time in despondency. No elevating faith tore into his stiff tongue and soothed his ears. The suction of the sea instilled no fear in him. No wonder occurred, nor had he the strength to wrench the boat away.

The chasm swallowed him.

And what the chasm takes in, it keeps.

It is death's faithful ally, and undisturbed as death swallows up the crumbling remains – at long intervals – without haste" …

Jussa folded his hands. "May God have mercy on the soul of the deaf and dumb stranger! Amen." ---

When Jussa stepped out of the sacristy, the strange woman was already sitting in the sleigh – far down on the road.

She herself was holding the reins. The horse wanted to go; but she held it back.

He stood immovable on the steps. His hand jerked and wanted to go up to his leather cap; but he wasn't able to lift it, and he languished during his soul's impotence …

She looked back.

Her chin bent more and more down toward her shoulder, but her eyes flowed up to him, and perhaps her blood flowed along; she turned pale … The horse jerked. She handed the reins to the driver. "Drive quickly!"

— Only when they swung down over the ice on the river did her face loosen to a trembling sigh, and the twinges quivered like shudders around her lips:

"Drive quickly!"

The comfort during the trip was interrupted every so often by an anxiety-filled feeling that something of a shadow, a thought of him was following in her wake. Yet one more time her senses are filled with the bewilderment of cruelty and with the desire to be embraced by him, who walked with loneliness around him … Was he following? … She had to look back. Again and again she had to look back; the enigmatic uncertainty began anew to bind her countenance …

But then she awakened again. "Drive quickly!"

… The sun ran into a break in the clouds and cast a reddening reflection onto the snowflakes that were beginning to fall gently down, at first spread out, then more dense, until the sun could no longer break through them.

… She sat prostrate beneath the bearskin pelt … Her little, blond boy wasn't going to have to ask any more when they would be traveling to Papa. Good God, things were so bad with her husband when "it began" in the autumn – in the autumn, when Juhani came and dammed up my memories. But she couldn't help it! And she had cried many times because she couldn't help it …

The fjord and sea came into view.

Her tears melted the snowflakes on her cheeks. "Juhani! I couldn't help it! God help me! I didn't know any better" …

— And she remembered what her mother on her deathbed had written in her album. It was written with Gothic letters.

"If you encounter a great disappointment in life, my child – and there is one that is the greatest of all disappointments, then do not believe that the pain of the first bitterness is sorrow.

Matti Aikio (1872-1929), a Sámi from Karasjok, Finnmark, Norway, was one of the world's earliest indigenous writers. His first Norwegian novel *In Reindeer Hide* came out in 1906 four years before Johan Turi's *An Account of the Sámi*. Turi wrote in Sámi (with some help from Emilie Demant), whereas Aikio, who did not begin studying Norwegian until he was eighteen, spent most of the rest of his relatively short life in Oslo writing in Norwegian. He wrote articles for newspapers and Christmas magazines as well as eight books of which six were novels. He was writing during a period of harsh assimilation and social Darwinism. His books were popular among Norwegians who were interested in the exotic people up north, but they were less successful among his own people, in part because he saw that the best way forward for the Sámi was to learn the majority language which was tantamount to his supporting assimilation. Cf. Gunnar Gjengset's article "Citizens and Nomads: The Literary Works of Matti Aikio with Emphasis on *Bygden på Elvenesset*," *Journal of Northern Studies* 1 * 2010, 45-65.

*

Dr. Elina Helander-Renvall from Ohcejohka, Finland is a Sámi scholar with many articles and books to her credit. Her research areas include Sámi customary law, traditional knowledge, traditional cultures and lifestyles of the Arctic and sustainable development. She also happens to be an excellent artist and produced the painting on this book's cover. For more of her work go to siida@samimuseum.fi

*

Hans Hansen Lilienskiold (ca.1650–1703) was a Norwegian civil servant and non-fiction writer born in Bergen. He was named County governor of Finnmark from 1684, moved with his family to Vardøhus in 1687 and a few months later to Vadsø, the largest commercial center in Finnmark. He is remembered for his works on the geography and culture of Finnmark especially *Speculum Boreale*, a regional topographical work describing the landscape, people and cultural history of Finnmark. My gratitude to Archives: Finnmark County Library for permission to use some of the illustrations from *Speculum Boreale* between the chapters of this book.